# KICK

# MITCH JOHNSON

USBORNE

# IT'S NOW OR NEVER

Two minutes left on the clock.

The crowd watch with their hands clasped on top of their heads. Scarves hang loosely around their necks. Some of them puff their cheeks out.

It's now or never.

The ball is chipped in from midfield and finds him on the edge of the box. He takes it down on his chest and sidesteps the incoming defender. He pulls his foot back to take a shot but dummies instead, cutting inside the next tackle.

The crowd rise to their feet as he surges into the box.

The defenders slide to try and stop his shot, but his touch has taken the ball beyond their reach. The goalkeeper steps forward, arms stretched wide, eyes fixed on the ball. The crowd watch through their fingers.

*Then he shoots.*

*The ball fires past the goalkeeper's fingertips. But for a split second – a heartbeat – it looks as though it might go over the crossbar. The crowd gasp. And then, as the ball hits the back of the net, they erupt.*

*Real Madrid are the new champions!*

I run off to celebrate and slide on my knees. The little stones on the ground scrape against my skin, and as I get up I feel blood trickling down my leg. I rattle the rusty corrugated fence so it sounds like thousands of fans jumping and cheering in the stands. The crumbling apartment blocks rise up like a stadium on every side, and I roar loud enough for even the deaf old men on the fifth floor to hear. I put my fingers and thumbs together to make the shape of a heart, and pound my chest where the Real Madrid badge should be. The Indonesian wonder kid strikes again!

The heart shape is my trademark celebration. Whenever Uston scores he crosses his chest and points to the sky, even though he's supposed to be Muslim. We keep telling him that Allah will be angry if he makes the sign of the cross, but Uston says it doesn't matter because he's only pretending. I still don't think it's worth the risk.

Rochy comes over and puts his arm around my shoulders.

"What a goal, Budi! You left them for dead!"

I look across the square at Uston and Widodo lying on the ground. The warm evening air is thick with dust from their sliding tackles, and it smells like money.

The square isn't technically a square, it's a quadrilateral quadrangle. I know this because Rochy told me. And Rochy is a genius. He went to school until he was thirteen so he knows pretty much everything, although a lot of it is useless stuff like quadrilateral quadrangles, ancient history and something he calls "physics". He told me recently that the universe is expanding, but I don't really understand what that means. He's tried to explain it, but I'm not a scientific genius like him, I'm a footballing genius like Kieran Wakefield. And one day I'm going to be a world-famous footballer like him, too. So normally I just nod and say cool and ask Rochy to tell me something interesting about football instead.

Fachry, the goalkeeper, leans against the corrugated fence we use as a goal, pulling a piece of plastic coating from the football. Fachry has to go in goal because he's

Catholic. Catholic is just a type of Christian – there's more than one type. They all support the same god (who isn't Allah) but still don't agree. It's like Manchester United and Manchester City. They don't agree on anything other than being from Manchester. Fachry doesn't like going in goal but it's four Muslims against one Catholic. Rochy says that's democracy, and you can't argue with democracy.

Behind the fence is where the bins are kept. On one of the balconies above the bins, a scrawny man watches us with his feet resting in a groove where the wall has crumbled away. The soles of his feet are black. He chews his nails and spits them over the wall. The smell of fried vegetables and spices wafts across the pitch. The clank of pots and pans reaches us from three sides of the square, but the far end is eerily quiet.

This is where the Dragon lives.

Some people think the Dragon is called the Dragon because he comes from Komodo, which is true but it's not the reason. Komodo is where they used to send all the criminals, so everyone who comes from there is descended from a convict. This explains a lot, but it isn't the reason why the Dragon is called the Dragon.

Other people think the Dragon is called the Dragon

because he looks like one. They say he got the nickname because of his big stomach and the jewelled rings he wears on every finger and the thick gold chains around his neck. In fact, he was called the Dragon before those things. His big belly and rings and chains are because he's rich. Mega-rich. Like a footballer. He's the main landlord and moneylender for the area, so everyone owes the Dragon something. And if you don't, it's probably because you just paid him.

The real reason why the Dragon got his nickname has got nothing to do with where he's from or how he looks. The Dragon is called the Dragon because if you cross him or betray him or bad-mouth him, he'll chew you up and spit out your bones. And he won't bother burying what's left of you, either.

As the dust settles it sticks to the sweat on my skin. Widodo is up on his feet, brushing the dirt from his shorts. When he offers to help his brother up, Uston slaps his hand away.

"Come on, Uston," Rochy says. "Don't be a sore loser."

"I want a rematch," Uston says, sitting up and hanging his head between his knees.

"It's too late now," Rochy says. "I have to get home."

"What about golden goal?"

"Forget it, Uston," I say. "You only have golden goal if the teams draw, and we beat you."

"Shut up, Budi, that goal was a fluke."

"No, it wasn't."

"Yes, it was! I bet if we play another match you won't score any. How about we play one-on-one: Barcelona versus Real Madrid? Fachry can stay in goal, and Rochy can run home to his mummy."

"What about me?" Widodo asks.

"You can referee," Uston says.

Widodo frowns and starts dusting his shorts again. You'd expect Uston to be a better loser by now – me and Rochy have given him plenty of practice – but I suppose anyone who thinks that *Barcelona* are better than Real Madrid must have a lot of problems. I really want to stay and beat him, but I know I shouldn't be late home for dinner.

"Budi!" Rochy shouts suddenly. "Your leg!"

I look down just as the trail of blood reaches my ankle. The drop spills over the plastic tongue of my boot and seeps into the laces. It's the most impressive injury I've ever had.

"Whoa! That's a nasty one," Rochy says. "You should go home and get that cleaned up."

The others gather round and admire the cut in my knee. When I bend my leg it feels sore, and a fresh dribble of blood seeps out.

"Yeah, you should go home," Fachry says.

I pick up my football and start hobbling home. It doesn't really hurt that much, but you've got to make the most of it. That's what footballers do. Above my head, washing lines droop between the buildings, and the clothes, bleached by the summer sun, are like Madrid flags. Like we've won La Liga. Like this is the homecoming.

My chest fills with pride, and I pat my T-shirt where the Real Madrid badge should be.

"I'll play you one-on-one tomorrow night, Uston," I call over my shoulder, breaking into a stiff jog. "Barca are going down!"

# THERE'S NO PLACE LIKE HOME

"**W**hat on earth have you done to your leg, Budi?"

Mum is always worrying. Worrying about Grandma, worrying about money, worrying about me. I'm always telling her that she shouldn't worry so much because it's bad for her health, but then she just worries about worrying. She gets especially worried whenever I cut myself, because I've got this condition where you don't stop bleeding. There's something wrong with my blood which means it doesn't clot properly. Uston says it's because my family don't pray or fast like proper Muslims, so Allah has cursed us. My grandpa had it, and my dad and his twin brother have it too, so it's kind of like a family curse. But we don't talk about my uncle. Not since he took a one-way trip to Execution Island.

What Uston doesn't realize is that having a bleeding problem makes you the best at dodging tackles, so it's actually a blessing.

"It's okay," I say. "It's just a graze."

"But there's blood everywhere!"

I look down and realize it looks a lot worse since I ran home. The blood has trickled round my shin, and there are spots of it all over my boots.

"How did it happen?"

"I got attacked by a tiger."

"Oh really?" She crosses her arms, creasing the orange fabric of her shirt. "And what was a tiger doing in the middle of Jakarta?"

"It must have swum all the way here from Sumatra. Rochy says that Sumatran tigers are really good swimmers because they've got webbed paws."

"Is that right?" Mum asks. "It must have been hungry to swim all that way."

"Very hungry."

"So why did it take such a small bite?"

"It ate Uston first."

Mum laughs, and I smile because all the worry disappears from her face. But then she looks very serious.

"I hope Uston isn't responsible for what happened to

your leg. I hope you boys are playing nicely. Doesn't Rochy look after you?"

That's the trouble with being small for your age – everyone thinks you need a bodyguard. Especially when you have a bleeding problem.

"I don't need looking after, Mum – I'm almost twelve. Anyway, you should have seen the goal I scored!"

She ruffles my hair. "You can tell me all about it over dinner. But first you need to clean up your leg before Dad gets home. Wait on the step and I'll bring you a cloth and some water."

Sitting in the doorway with my legs stretched out into the street, I pick at the crusty blood on the front of my shin. I dig out a small chunk of glass from the skin beneath my knee and flick it across the road. It lands among some rubbish in the doorway of the crumbling apartment block opposite. The block has been on the verge of collapsing for as long as I can remember – the walls have wide cracks sprouting from the floor, and the whole thing seems to lean towards the building next to it. Dad says they used the wrong type of concrete and the government has banned everyone from living there. But the Dragon still rents it out.

Mum brings the cloth and water and puts them down

next to me. The printed flowers on the hem of her *kain* swish across the ground, and she makes the dust smell like flowers too.

"Make sure you wash all the grit out. If it gets infected I don't know how we'll pay for medication."

Mum goes back into the apartment and I start washing the spots of blood from my boots because I don't want them to get stained. Mum and Dad bought them for my birthday last year and I've finally grown into them. They're fakes, obviously, but they're good fakes. Real fakes. I know they must have been expensive, and the last thing I want is to have bloodstained football boots. You never see a professional footballer in bloodstained boots, do you?

After I've finished cleaning my boots I start scrubbing at my shin. The blood comes off pretty easily, and by the time Dad arrives I've washed all the little bits of grit out of the cut.

Dad works in a factory that makes smart shirts for businessmen, and even though he doesn't have to, he always wears a short-sleeved shirt with a collar to work – either his white one or the one with yellow and blue checks. He says it's important to be proud of yourself. He's always telling me: "Budi, if you don't respect

yourself, nobody will. You must be proud of who you are."
Today he's wearing the shirt with yellow and blue checks,
and it sticks to a sweaty patch on his chest. As he gets
closer he smiles and sits down on the step beside me.

"What's happened here then?" he asks, kissing me on
the head.

"I cut my leg playing football."

Dad leans over and grimaces as I show him my knee.
The cut glistens with fresh blood. "Make sure you get all
the grit out. We don't want it to get infected."

I nod and keep brushing it with the cloth.

"Was it a foul?" Dad asks.

"No, but I scored an amazing goal, so it was worth
it."

"Good boy! If you keep it up you'll play for Madrid
one day."

"*Real* Madrid, Dad. If you just say Madrid it could
mean Atlético Madrid, and I would rather never play
football again than play for them."

"I know, I know. I meant Real Madrid. Just keep
practising and you'll get there."

I smile and Dad pats me on the back. It's already dark
but the air is still very warm. Dad looks up at the small
patches of sky among the laundry.

16

"It's going to rain soon," he says. "The monsoon must be on its way. Can you feel it?"

"Yeah," I say, but at the moment it's hard to imagine the bone-dry streets thick with mud, rainwater dripping from the empty washing lines, and people splashing through puddles with newspapers held above their heads. Sometimes it feels like the dry season will never end, that the days will just get hotter and hotter for ever. But it's got to rain soon. The air has become sticky and heavy waiting for it. But tonight there are no clouds, just a black, starless sky, so the weather won't break yet.

The sound of people chattering over dinner reaches us from the apartments above. Every so often a scooter blares past, kicking up dust that turns red in the glow of the brake lights.

A fresh trickle of blood dribbles down my shin.

"Here," Dad says, taking a handkerchief from his pocket and twisting it. "Hold this against your knee while I knot it."

He ties the bandage tight.

"How's that?"

"Much better."

My stomach rumbles and he smiles. "Come on, let's go and see if dinner's ready."

Mum is just spooning the rice onto steel trays when we walk in, and I help her carry them from the kitchen in one corner to the table in the other. Grandma is already waiting with a blanket wrapped around her shoulders.

"Hello, Grandma," I say. "Aren't you going to be hot in that blanket? You know Mum's made spicy *rendang* tonight."

Mum hasn't really made spicy *rendang*, because today is Wednesday. On Wednesdays we just have rice. Wednesdays are better than Fridays because we don't have anything on Fridays. But I like to imagine there's a feast on the rickety little table and Grandma plays along. Tonight it's a tray of Mum's world-famous *rendang*.

"I'm just fine, thank you," Grandma says. "An old woman like me needs to keep warm. And I haven't tasted a *rendang* that's been too spicy for me yet!"

When Grandma smiles her wrinkly face creases even more, and her eyes become narrow slits. Grandma isn't like other old ladies, because most of them get really thin and bony the older they get, but Grandma still has plump, round cheeks. She puts this down to "maintaining a healthy appetite", which is almost as important as "being proud of who you are" and "pursuing your dreams".

Grandma is full of useful advice and interesting stories. Once a snake bit her on the arm and she sucked the venom out. Now she is immune to venom. Another time, she fell from a third-storey window but landed in a passing cart carrying silks and soft fabrics. It's because of this, and the fact that she is the oldest person I know, that I'm beginning to think Grandma might be indestructible.

"Your mother was just telling me that you cut your leg today. I hope you washed it properly."

"Yes, Grandma. I got all the grit out."

"And I suppose I'd never be able to guess how you hurt yourself…"

"Playing football!"

"Football. Always football. Football will be the death of you, young man."

Grandma smiles at me, and for a moment I think she is going to come clean about being indestructible, but then she looks down at her tray and takes a big mouthful of rice. I know she's joking about football being the death of me, because being a footballer is probably the safest job in the world. When a footballer gets injured there are about six doctors around him in a second, even if he's just pretending. Once I waited almost six hours to see a doctor at the hospital when Mum thought I was bleeding on the inside, and even then I didn't get put on a stretcher and carried about like a prince.

Bleeding on the inside is the worst. Most people think having a bleeding problem means you're going to bleed to death from the tiniest cut, but the real problem is bleeding on the inside. At any moment I might start bleeding and not know until I fall over and die. You can't see it. You can't taste it. Some people can't even feel it, but I think I can. It's that feeling like when you've done something bad and Grandma or Rochy find out, and there's a knife in you somewhere, near your heart, and with every word they say it turns a little further, pushing in a little deeper. Bleeding on the inside is definitely the worst.

Mum turns to Dad and says, "How was work today, Elvis?"

That's another thing about Grandma: she gave Dad a crazy name. Elvis Presley was an American singer and movie star about sixty years ago, and Grandma was madly in love with him until he died on the toilet. I suppose it's hard to love someone after that. But while he was still alive Dad was born and Grandma called him Elvis. I'm not sure how Grandpa felt about the whole situation. I would ask him but I can't because he died in a big earthquake that happened when I was little. Mum says I slept through the whole thing.

It suddenly hits me that I don't know what Grandma called my uncle. If she had twins and named one of them Elvis, what did she call the other one? Presley? Without thinking, I interrupt Dad telling us about his day and ask Grandma.

"Grandma, what name did you give to Uncle?"

I should have remembered this silence from the last time I mentioned Uncle in front of my family. I should have remembered the stern look on Grandma's face. The coolness in her eyes. That feeling like her hand is gripping the knife on the inside. Slowly, she turns her head to face me.

"Budi," she says, "you don't have an uncle. Not any more."

I swallow, even though there's nothing in my mouth.

"Yes, Grandma," I mutter, but I still don't understand. I mean, obviously they call Nusa Kambangan "Execution Island" for a reason. I know what happens there. I know no one comes back. I know when you do something wrong, something bad, they take you there and lock you up in a tiny cell for years and years until you're sure everyone has forgotten about you. Then one night, while you're asleep on your flea-ridden bed, they drag you out to a quiet place, kicking and screaming and confused, and they give you a choice: kneeling or standing?

And then they shoot you.

No matter how much you beg and cry and plead – no matter how blurry your vision gets, or how much your nose runs – they aim their rifles at your heart and shoot you.

I know all that. I have nightmares about it.

What I don't know is whether Uncle has been there long enough yet.

And my family aren't going to tell me.

I stare into my tray and chew a mouthful of rice for as long as it takes for someone to break the silence.

"Sorry," Mum says, talking to Dad but looking at me, "you were telling us about your day, Elvis."

"You know how frustrating it is," Dad says. "I asked Supardi when we'll be getting last month's wages, and he said it should be any day now. But I know he's too scared to confront the boss about it. I don't blame him – he knows if he makes a fuss it will probably delay the payment even more. He might even lose his job if he upsets the wrong people. But it's annoying, especially because I'm still waiting for overtime from the month before that."

Mum reaches across to Dad and strokes his arm.

"It'll be a lot easier when the minimum wage goes up," she says.

"If it ever goes up!" says Grandma. "They talk about these things all the time but nothing seems to happen. And those people protesting in the streets will only make things worse, no matter what they say."

Dad takes a deep breath and his face breaks into a smile. "Come now, *Ibu*. Change is coming. Things *will* get easier. Besides, we'll be rich when Budi plays for Real Madrid."

Dad winks at me and Grandma shakes her head, muttering something about football.

"Tell us about the goal you scored today, Budi," Mum says.

"I'll have to stand up to explain it properly."

"Don't get indigestion," Mum says.

"I won't."

I do them an action replay. I show them how Rochy chipped the ball to me, how I took it down on my chest, dodged Widodo's tackle, dummied the shot, stepped inside Uston, and scored past Fachry. It's hard to do the goal justice in such a small space, but my family clap as I run round the table celebrating. I have to stop to squeeze between Dad's chair and the wall, but when I get through

I put my fingers and thumbs together to make the shape of a heart, and pat my chest where the Real Madrid badge should be.

"I wish I could have seen it," Grandma says, smiling.

"When I'm a professional I'll buy you a television so you can watch me play without leaving your armchair."

They all laugh, but suddenly Grandma starts coughing horribly. It sounds like rocks are being grated inside her throat, and bits of rice fly from her mouth. Mum gets up and pats her on the back, but Grandma holds up a hand to make her stop.

I try to ignore Grandma's coughing fit by scraping the last of my rice into a pile. I hate looking at Grandma when she's coughing. Her eyes become all bloodshot and tears roll over her cheeks. It's like she becomes a different person. Someone who is not indestructible. But after a minute or so she always recovers and tries to pretend nothing has happened, even though her eyes are red and watery, and the squiggly vein on her forehead bulges beneath her skin.

"I'll watch every match you play in," she says, as Mum lifts a cup of water to her lips.

We finish dinner and I help Mum clear the trays away. Dad gives Grandma his arm so she can get back to her armchair. I don't like watching Grandma on the move because she always looks so weak. When she is sitting in her big cosy armchair with a blanket across her lap, smiling at everything and telling stories about her youth, she doesn't seem that old. But when she shuffles across the room with her back hunched over, she starts to look like the old beggar women who roam the streets. It's only a couple of metres from the table to her chair, but she makes it seem like a marathon. That's why I'm always so keen to help with the washing-up after dinner: by the time I turn round again, Grandma is tucked up in her chair.

"Will you tell me a story, Grandma, before I go to bed?"

"Of course, come and sit on the rug and I'll tell you about the time I found a tiger in the yard."

"No, Grandma, tell me a story that I haven't heard before."

"Okay, let me see. Have I told you about the time it rained so hard the roof collapsed?"

"Yes."

"How about the man I knew with six fingers and six toes?"

"Yes."

She scratches her neck and puts a finger to her lips.

Mum and Dad sit at the table, watching Grandma with smiling eyes.

"How about the boy I knew who wanted to be an actor?"

"No, you've never told me that one before. What happened?"

"Well, when I was a girl I knew a boy who wanted desperately to be an actor. He was a few years older than me – *very* good looking – and all he could think about was acting. When you talked to him, you would think nothing else existed. He said he wanted to be a famous actor in the Hollywood movies. Everyone laughed at him, of course, because he worked in his father's paddy fields, didn't speak any English, and no one in the village had ever left the island, let alone been to America.

"But he didn't let that bother him. He used to save every rupiah he could, and when he had enough he would take the bus to the nearest town with a cinema and watch whatever was showing. He would come back full of energy and renewed ambition, determined to become a star. He could remember lines from the films, and would act them out if you asked him politely. I must say, he *was* very good. Then he would begin saving his money to do it all over again."

Grandma clasps her hands together and rests them on her lap. While she talks, I wind the tassels at the edge of the rug around my fingers. Apparently the rug was given to Grandma as a wedding gift, so it must be ancient. The patch in front of her chair is threadbare and not as soft as the rest, but it's still my favourite place to sit.

"And then what happened?" I ask.

"Well, one morning the boy's father went out into the fields to check the oxen had been rigged up to the plough for the day's work, but his son was nowhere to be seen. At first everyone thought he had taken an early bus to watch a film, and the farmer was furious at his son's negligence. But he still hadn't returned by mid-afternoon. When nightfall came the farmer remained adamant that his son would be back soon. He thought the boy was hiding nearby, planning to sneak back home after everyone had gone to bed to avoid being beaten. But night came and went, and gradually we came to realize he wasn't coming back."

Grandma stops to smooth the blanket across her lap. She always pauses at the worst moments.

"And then what happened?"

"The village never heard of him again – at least as far as I know, because I moved away a few years later.

27

Everyone assumed he had been kidnapped. People went missing all the time back then, more so than today. But then one day – it must have been about twenty years after he went missing – I was on a bus and I went past one of those big billboards just outside the city that was advertising a new American film. I couldn't be certain, because I only saw it for a few seconds before we drove by, but one of the actors looked just like an older version of the boy I knew! Well, I thought, that settles it. He did make it after all. I just hope he went back to visit his poor father once in a while."

"Are you sure it was him, Grandma?"

"Quite sure," she says, adjusting herself in her armchair. "I never forget a face."

"What was his name?"

"Don't ask me that! I might not forget a face, but I can certainly forget a name. Now, I can feel my eyelids drooping, and you've got an early start in the morning, so off you go to bed."

I get up and kiss Grandma on the cheek. Despite how wrinkled her face is, her skin is really soft.

"You'd better let your mother take a look at that cut," Grandma says, glancing down at the bloody bandage around my knee.

Mum gets up from the table and unties the handkerchief. It's soaked and hangs like a dead animal in her hand.

"It still looks fresh," she says. "Elvis, can you pass me the coconut butter?"

Dad retrieves a tin from the kitchen cupboard and passes it to Mum. She scoops out a dollop of butter and smears it across the cut with her fingertips. The coolness of it makes my knee twitch, and it's almost worth getting injured just for the sweet, delicious smell. Sometimes, when no one is looking, I eat the butter straight out of the tin to heal any cuts on the inside.

"There," she says, standing up and giving me a hug. "That should do the trick."

"We'll see you in the morning, superstar," Dad says, ruffling my hair. "Sleep well, son."

I go to my room and get undressed. The light bulb has gone so I have to do it in the dark, but it isn't difficult to find my mattress because it takes up most of the room.

When I'm in bed I listen to the hum of different generators, until one by one they're switched off, and I fall asleep to the distant sounds of the city.

# BIG BOSS MAN

**K**ieran Wakefield is my favourite player of all time. He is also the best player in the world. You can tell he is the best because Real Madrid paid more money for him than any club has paid for anyone else, ever. My dream is to see him play at the Bernabéu. That's where Real Madrid play their home matches. It can hold over 80,000 people and one day I want to be one of them.

I dream about Kieran Wakefield most days at the factory. My job is fairly repetitive so sometimes I go into a trance and think about how amazing he is at football, and what he might be doing while I'm sewing boots together. He's probably playing football, I know, but it's still nice to imagine. Rochy moans that he can't get through to me when I'm daydreaming, but I think he's just jealous because his favourite player, León Belmonte, isn't as good as Kieran Wakefield. They're both *Galácticos* but Wakefield cost more. Rochy says *Galácticos* just means superstars.

Rochy always wears a pink Manchester United shirt to work with *BELMONTE* on the back. Manchester United shirts should be red, but Rochy's is so old it's faded to pink. He doesn't actually support Manchester United any more because Belmonte plays for Real Madrid now, but it's his best shirt. Some people think you have to support the same team for ever, and that if you change teams you're a "glory supporter", but following your favourite player is different. Glory supporting is probably the ugliest thing about the beautiful game. Or maybe that's diving. Uston has started diving because his favourite player, Jesus Puga, does a lot of it. It's really disgraceful. But because we don't have a referee, he normally just gets kicked by whoever is nearest and told to get up.

"Budi!" Rochy shouts. "Hey, I'm going to start throwing things at you if you keep ignoring me!"

"I didn't hear you!" I shout back. The sewing machines are really loud sometimes. "What do you want?"

Rochy looks over both shoulders before shouting, "Did you hear that Wakefield is injured?"

"No, he isn't! Stop lying!"

"I'm not lying! I saw it on the television this morning!"

It's true that Rochy has a television – his dad bought it a long time ago. There's a crack that runs right down the middle of the screen so they can't sell it, but it still works. I'm supposed to be watching the Real Madrid v. Valencia match at his apartment tonight. It's also true that Rochy knows a lot about football. He's a few years older than me so he knows stuff that I'm too young to remember. I don't believe that Kieran Wakefield is injured though. I don't want to.

"I still think you're lying!"

"Whatever! You'll see later!"

The foreman approaches our row and we put our heads down. All I can think of is Kieran Wakefield rolling around on the floor holding his ankle. It's probably broken in three places and he'll never play again. It's a tragedy. Everyone will be wearing black armbands at the game tonight in honour of the best player in the world…

The foreman stops at my station and taps his *rotan* on the workbench.

"Faster, Budi! Faster!"

I can smell coffee and cigarettes on his breath. I work faster. Even though I don't look round I can sense him waiting behind me, and the skin on the back of my arms tingles in anticipation of the *rotan*.

The foreman doesn't know about my bleeding problem. I think maybe it's not just words that can make you bleed on the inside. And I think the foreman knows that too.

Slow beads of sweat roll down the sides of my face, gathering beneath my chin and dripping into my lap. My shirt sticks to my back. His presence is distracting, so I try to think of something else.

*Kieran Wakefield hobbles to the side of the pitch and shakes his head. He makes the sign for a substitution. The bench look worried. Everyone in the crowd acts like Real Madrid are about to be relegated...*

My fingertips are sweaty and the plastic upper slips every time I push it towards the needle. It's normally only when I'm really tired at the end of a shift that I start making mistakes, but we haven't even reached our lunch break yet. Another stale gust of coffee and cigarette smoke fills my nostrils. I wonder whether the foreman was just sighing, or whether the air stirred because he moved his hand, aiming the *rotan* at the soft flesh on the back of my arm. I can't even tell whether he's still standing behind me, the air is so thick with the buzzing of machines. My fingers slip again, but I manage to keep the stitches straight.

I try to imagine the foreman isn't there. I tell myself that this pair of boots is the pair that Kieran Wakefield will make his comeback in. I really concentrate on making them the best boots I've ever made and focus on every stitch.

As well as making boots for Kieran Wakefield, we also make boots for Lazaro Celestino, who is probably the most overrated player of all time. He plays for Barcelona, which says it all really. Sometimes when I'm making his boots I deliberately miss a few stitches just to annoy him.

Stitching the upper is the most important job in the factory because that's the part you use to kick the ball. If there's a crease in the material the consequences could be disastrous. Someone might end up missing a penalty in the World Cup Final. It could literally change the course of history. The upper is also the part you see most on television, and it would look pretty bad if a professional footballer kept tripping over loose thread.

The upper arrives in different pieces that are cut out by a big blue machine standing against the far wall. These pieces are all different colours: red, green, pink, yellow, orange. Rochy swears that once upon a time all football boots were black, which must have been really boring. We then sew all these pieces together in a particular order. The foreman gets really angry if we make a mistake, so we have to be careful. He also gets really angry if we're too slow, so we have to be fast. He's kind of like a referee who can't stand late tackles or time-wasting, but instead of yellow cards he uses the *rotan*, and instead of red cards he throws people out on the street. The strictest referee in the world. The Referee of Doom.

Another stale breath reminds me that the strictest referee in the world is watching my every move, and so I think of something else before I make a mistake.

After we've stitched the upper, another section of workers glues the upper to the sole unit. If the boot has studs, a machine screws them in. If the machine is broken, a person screws them in. Once I took too long on a toilet break (I had diarrhoea) and the foreman made me screw studs into boots for the rest of the afternoon. It's the second worst job in the factory, and it's made even worse when your stomach hurts so much that you think you might *berak* at any moment.

After that the boots have insoles put in and labels attached. Then they're laced up by a section of girl ninjas.

I call them ninjas because they're silent and lightning fast and most of them wear black headscarves.

Finally, the boots are inspected before being wrapped in paper and boxed up. Boxing shoes is the worst job in the factory. It's also the easiest job in the world, and only the real idiots work on that section. Being moved from sewing to boxing is like being substituted at half-time. And not because you've already scored a hat-trick and need to be rested for the midweek cup fixture, but because you're rubbish. Once I was late because I had to help Mum with Grandma in the morning, and the foreman put me on boxing for a week as punishment. It was so boring. I haven't been late since.

The buzzer suddenly goes for break and makes me jump. Luckily I don't mess up the stitching. The slight shadow over my station disappears, and from the corner of my eye I watch the foreman stroll along the row. Every few steps he leans over someone's shoulder, readjusting his grip on the *rotan*, before nodding and moving on.

Because Rochy and I work on the same section we don't normally get the same break, which is really annoying because I want to know if he is joking or whether Kieran Wakefield actually is injured. I tell myself that he probably isn't injured, and if he is it's probably something minor. He can't be seriously injured because everything seems too normal. If something terrible had happened, I'd feel it. I'd just know.

I place the finished upper on the pile next to my machine and head upstairs to the canteen. The canteen is a stuffy little room that overlooks the factory, where a scrawny lady in an apron serves mushy rice and "Sauce of the Day".

"Sauce of the Day" is the same every day, and I think it tastes like cabbage and coconut. Some people say it tastes like beansprouts and coconut. Other people say it tastes like cigarette ash and coconut, which would make sense because it's grey and the serving lady always has a cigarette hanging from her lip. Whatever it is, it's definitely coconut-based.

Everyone in the canteen seems interested in only one thing: the pay rise. At the next table, a group of women talk excitedly about the extra money they'll earn when the minimum wage goes up. One of them says that she'll be able to afford more food for her children. Another says that she might be able to start paying off her brother's debts. A younger girl says she might be able to afford to go to school again.

That's another thing I don't like about the canteen –

everyone suffers from a total lack of imagination. Maybe if you eat enough "Sauce of the Day" it goes to your brain. When I get the pay rise, I'm going to the Bernabéu, not wasting it on the boring stuff people spend money on every day.

One of the women tells the others not to get so excited.

"This money will never materialize," she says, looking into her tray of grey rice. "It's all just talk and nonsense."

"But it's been agreed by the government," one of the others says.

"So what? The government says it's going to do lots of things, but do they ever get done? They always talk about new hospitals and schools and jobs, but that's all it is – talk. I haven't seen anything change for years. This is just a new tactic to make the protestors go back to work. Even if there is an increase in the minimum wage, it'll be years before we get it, and by that time everything will have gone up in price so we won't be any better off."

The rest of the women look pretty unhappy when she finally stops talking, but I know she's got it wrong. After all, Dad reads the newspaper every day, so he knows what's going on. The women look so miserable that I feel like telling them not to worry, but then something catches my eye outside the window.

On the walkway above the factory, one of the Dragon's brothers approaches the foreman's office. The last time I counted, the Dragon had three brothers, although new ones are always turning up from Komodo and old ones are always disappearing. They all look the same – fat and rich and mean. Once the Dragon found out that one of his brothers was taking an extra cut from the rent collections. So the Dragon killed him. Well, he cut his fingers off first. Then he killed him and dumped the body in one of the bins in the square, about thirty metres from where he lives. Everyone knows the Dragon did it, but no one went to the police because one of the Dragon's other brothers is the Chief Inspector. And only an idiot would arrest his brother for being a brother murderer.

The brother that's on the walkway goes straight into the foreman's office without knocking, and he emerges a few minutes later with a thick brown envelope. Rochy says that even though the factory is outside the Dragon's territory, he's always threatening to burn it to the ground, so the foreman has to pay him protection money. The Dragon's brother flicks through the contents of the envelope before tucking it into his back pocket. As he turns to leave he catches my eye, and before I have the sense to stare down into my tray of grey rice he winks at me and smiles, showing off the gaps between his stained teeth.

I don't look up from my tray for the rest of my break. I just scrape the stodgy rice into my mouth and force it down. Only someone with a death wish looks one of the Dragon's Clan in the eye.

When the buzzer goes I return to my station and find Rochy hunched over his machine. There is a dark patch around the number seven on his back. Some of the curved lettering at the top of the shirt is beginning to peel away. He looks up as I start sewing, and the beads of sweat glisten on his forehead.

"It's too hot today!" he shouts, rubbing a hand over his face.

"And too loud!" I say.

The foreman comes out of his office and stands on the walkway overlooking the factory floor. Rochy and I both concentrate on our work until he goes back inside.

"Hey, Budi!"

"What?"

"Did you know that top footballers only wear a pair of boots three times?"

"No! Is that true?"

"Yeah, they wear them for two training sessions to get

used to them, and then wear them for one match!"

"Then what do they do with them?"

"I don't know – probably throw them away!"

Now, Rochy knows a lot about football, but that is definitely not true. If that were true it would hardly be worth the effort of making them. I imagine there are probably fans like me who collect them, or the players in lower leagues get to use them, or there is a big boot-shaped museum that displays them all. If I manage to save enough money I would like to visit that museum, as well as seeing Kieran Wakefield play at the Bernabéu. I'll probably take my whole family, including Grandma.

"Maybe that's why they get paid so much money!" I say.

Rochy looks up from the boot he's stitching. "What?"

"Maybe footballers get paid a lot because they have to buy a new pair of boots every week!"

Rochy shakes his head. "Footballers don't buy their own boots!"

I'm pretty sure that is wrong too. If footballers don't buy their own boots, then who does? Their parents? I want to ask Rochy who pays for footballers' boots, but I don't want to look stupid, so I just keep stitching. I also want to ask him how much it would cost to see Kieran

Wakefield play at the Bernabéu, but then the foreman comes out of his office and starts pacing along the walkway, tapping his *rotan* against the railing…

# 11 REASONS WHY KIERAN WAKEFIELD IS BETTER THAN LAZARO CELESTINO

1. No one has ever paid 150 million euros for Lazaro Celestino.
2. Kieran Wakefield is taller, which means he is better at headers.
3. Being bigger also means he is better at tackling.
4. And shielding the ball.
5. Being taller means that if the goalkeeper gets sent off and the manager has already made all three substitutions, Kieran Wakefield would be a good stand-in goalkeeper.
6. Kieran Wakefield is really quick – probably quicker than Lazaro Celestino.
7. Kieran Wakefield is stronger.
8. Kieran Wakefield is younger.
9. Kieran Wakefield plays for a team who have won more Champions League titles than Lazaro Celestino's team.
10. Kieran Wakefield plays for a team who have won more La Liga titles than Lazaro Celestino's team.

11. Kieran Wakefield wears the number 11 shirt, which is my favourite number and one better than Lazaro Celestino's number 10.

# FROM RAGS TO RICHES

At the end of the day I have to shield my eyes from the sun when I leave. There aren't any windows in the factory, only long electric strip lights, so it always seems really bright when you step outside, even just before sunset. It doesn't help that everything in the factory (apart from the multicoloured boots) is grey, or made greyish by a layer of dust, and it takes a minute for my eyes to adjust to all the colours of the street.

The road outside the factory is always busy with scooters and cars. People beep their horns for no reason. The air above the traffic is blurred by pollution, and the distant skyscrapers sparkle and shimmer through the haze as though they're made of water. When the pollution gets really bad the lights of the city form a kind of halo in the evening, as though there are two setting suns – one in the west and one in the south.

Even though Rochy lives to the north, near the slums, he walks back with me, weaving in and out of the masses of people going to and from work. Some of them crowd around stalls, scooping delicious street food into their mouths. The spicy, salty smell is enough to make me stop and breathe it in, but Rochy grabs my arm and pulls me along. We take a shortcut down an alleyway and stop at the building where Uston and Widodo live.

"Hey, Barca scum!" I shout at the top-floor window. "We're ready for that rematch!"

Almost immediately their mum puts her head out of the window, and from the expression on her face I think she might be a Barcelona fan.

"Who do you think you are," she says, "coming here and hollering abuse in the street? I should come down there and teach you some manners!" She disappears but is back at the window in an instant. We have to duck out of the way as a heavy vegetable root flies towards us.

"We're sorry, *Ibu*," Rochy says. "We just want to know if Uston and Widodo are there?"

"No," she says. "They must have been kept late. Now get going before I find something else to throw at you!"

Rochy and I walk away. Uston and Widodo work at another factory with Fachry. Sometimes if the factory is behind or has a big order, everyone has to work overtime to catch up. It's the same at the factory where Rochy and I work, although the foreman has a way of making sure everything is done on time.

"I might go home if the others aren't around," Rochy says. "See you for the match tonight?"

"I'll be there."

Rochy turns down the next alley and I start dribbling a stone along the street, imagining that every passer-by is a Valencia defender trying to stop me as I race towards goal. I'm almost home when I remember to stop at a stall to buy Grandma's medicine and cigarettes. Then I carry on, kicking the stone into the centre of the road and firing it into the littered doorway of the apartment building opposite.

I make the shape of a heart with my fingers and pat my chest where the Real Madrid badge should be.

When I get home Grandma is asleep in her armchair, snoring quietly. Mum is cooking in the corner, and she looks over her shoulder as I walk into the room.

"Did you get the cigarettes and medicine?" she asks.

I lift up the blue plastic bag and put it on the table.

Even though Mum has to shout over the sizzling vegetables in the pan, Grandma doesn't wake up. This is another of her secrets for indestructibility: "Sleep as much as you can." I know cats that don't sleep as much as Grandma. She can even sleep through the calls to prayer that blare out from the nearby mosque five times a day.

"Can you wake Grandma up?" Mum says, stirring the vegetables. "Dinner is almost ready and she needs to take her tablets."

The best way to wake Grandma up is to shake her gently by the shoulder. She doesn't like it if you make a sudden loud noise, or squirt water in her face, or pinch her nose so she can't breathe. I've tried all those once before.

"Wake up, Grandma," I whisper. "Time for your tablets."

Gradually she lifts her head and blinks a few times.

"Hello, Budi," she says. Her breath is always really sour just after she's woken up. "Is it that time already? Will you get them out of the packet for me? They're ever so fiddly."

I fetch a cup of water and push two of the tablets out into Grandma's palm.

"Thank you." She gulps the tablets down and hands the cup back to me. "Could you pass me a cigarette too?"

"We're about to eat," Mum calls. "Are you sure you want to smoke now?"

"What are we having?" Grandma asks.

"Just vegetables and rice – we can't really afford to buy meat until Elvis gets paid."

Grandma shakes her head. "Shouldn't he be home by now?"

"Yes," Mum says, scraping rice onto separate trays. "But he said this morning the factory might be kept open for longer. Something about a new contract."

Grandma is still shaking her head. "He already works too much. Can't he turn the overtime down?"

"I don't know," Mum says, topping the rice with vegetables. "But we could really use the extra cash."

"That's if they pay him for it," Grandma says, rolling her eyes.

Mum shrugs and carries the trays to the table. "Budi, can you help Grandma, please?"

Grandma grips my wrist as she stands, and I guide her to the table. It's not as bad as watching Dad help her because I can't really tell how hunched over she is, and I can feel the strength in her hands.

"We'll have to start without your father," Mum says as I sit down next to her. "I'm sure he'll be back soon."

But he still hasn't come home four hours later. His untouched tray of cold, wet vegetables and rice sits on the rickety table. Grandma is smoking her third cigarette since dinner in her armchair, and the room is hazy with smoke. Mum sews a button onto Dad's white shirt, but she keeps glancing at the empty doorway.

"I don't like not knowing where he is," she says.

"Don't worry," Grandma says, exhaling two jets of smoke from her nostrils. "He'll be at the factory."

"Grandma," I say, "why do you smoke?"

She takes another drag and taps her cigarette over the chipped ashtray.

"Back when I started, they used to think smoking was good for you. Everyone I knew smoked, even though none of us could really afford it. And Elvis smoked too – the singer, I mean, not your father. He used to smoke cigars, but they've always been too expensive, so I smoked cigarettes instead."

"But doesn't smoking make your cough worse?"

Grandma blows a long cloud of smoke – like she's trying to whistle – before crushing the cigarette in the ashtray.

"Yes, it does," she says. "But I can't give up now. I'm too old to change."

Grandma closes her eyes and rests her head against the back of the chair. Mum squints at the shirt across her lap, trying to sew in the dim light. Outside, scooters come and go constantly. That's the problem with living on an island, even one as big as Java – you can only go so far before you have to stop and turn back. That's why everyone here goes round in circles. Unless you own a boat as well. But there are so many islands in Indonesia that you'd probably just end up on another one, driving round in circles again.

Suddenly Mum sighs loudly and lets the needle fall into her lap.

"It's no good," she says, "I have to know what's going on. Budi, will you go to the factory for me and tell your father to come home immediately? You can go to Rochy's straight after."

"Okay," I say, getting to my feet and heading for the door.

"And don't stay up too late," she calls after me. "Remember you have work in the morning."

Outside the air is really warm and still. Scooters using our street as a cut-through swerve around people and potholes. A little boy squats at the roadside, pushing litter into a burning pile with a stick and watching me as I pass. My nostrils sting with the smell of burning plastic. As I turn the corner I almost walk straight into someone coming the opposite way. I recognize the yellow and blue checks instantly.

"Hello, son," Dad says. His face glistens with sweat, and his damp shirt sticks to his chest. "What are you doing out here?"

"Mum sent me to look for you. She was getting worried."

"I thought she might send a search party. We got a new order so I had to work late. We must have made enough shirts for all the men in England!" Dad wipes his face with the back of his hand. "Anyway, let's go home. Your mother will be twice as worried now that you're out looking for me."

"Actually I'm going to Rochy's to watch the game."

"Yes, of course. Who are they playing tonight?"

"Valencia."

"Any good?"

"They're no match for Real Madrid. Kieran Wakefield will probably get a hat-trick."

"Well, let's hope so. Have fun, and say hello to Rochy's family for me."

Dad squeezes my shoulder and sets off home. He walks slowly, and the boy squatting by the roadside gets up and holds out his hand. Dad stops and shows his empty palms, and the boy goes back to sorting through the rubbish with a stick.

Rochy lives about twenty minutes away, and by the time I get there the roads are much quieter. Rochy's apartment is in the middle of a maze of narrow streets that people are always getting lost and robbed in. It's a good idea to walk with your pockets turned out so everyone can see you don't have anything to steal, even if you do look a bit silly.

Sometimes I feel really sorry for Rochy, because he has to share just one room with his mum and two older sisters. Imagine having two sisters – what a nightmare. Luckily they work as *pemulung*, and everyone knows the best time to scavenge is late in the evening – before the rats find anything worth eating – so Rochy doesn't have to put up with them too often. His mum is always at home though. She must be half Grandma's age but somehow she looks older. She never seems happy to see me, but Rochy tells me she never seems happy to see anyone. I think she's still sad about her husband dying, even though it happened over a year ago. Back then they used to live in a much bigger place, because Rochy's dad was a successful salesman. Apparently it even had a toilet – the type you sit on. But then his dad died and they had to move into a one-room apartment and Rochy had to leave school to come and work at the factory.

At first he was slow.

Unbelievably slow.

Lazaro Celestino slow.

I had to show him how to work faster, otherwise he would have been fired. I even gave him some of my uppers to make up his quota. The foreman was hard on him for the first few weeks. He used to say: "Why do you work so slowly, Rochy? Aren't you used to working hard? Your problem is that you think you're better than everyone else because you've had an education. You've been living the easy life. Don't hold it like that, you idiot! Hold it like this! It's not a pencil, you moron! Watch Budi, he knows what he's doing. If you haven't improved by the end of the week, I'm kicking your ass out of here! Then where will you be?"

At first Rochy didn't like me much, probably because the foreman kept telling him how slow he was compared to me. But Rochy is a really fast learner and within a month he was one of the best on the section. Then the foreman lost interest and found someone else to pick on.

When I discovered Rochy used to play for his school football team, I invited him to play with me and Uston and Fachry and Widodo, and after that he asked whether I wanted to watch the football at his apartment. Now we watch the Real Madrid matches as often as we can, although sometimes his mum tells him he's not allowed to invite anyone over, and sometimes the illegal satellite dish on the roof doesn't work.

When I arrive, Rochy's mum is already asleep on the mattress in the corner of the room. Rochy sits cross-legged on the floor in front of the television. There is a pile of pumpkin seed shells in front of him, and as I sit down he offers me a handful of seeds.

"Is Kieran Wakefield on the squad list?" I ask, chewing a seed and spitting out the shell.

"Yeah, they're just warming up now. I was only joking about him being injured."

Rochy looks at me and grins. Even though Kieran Wakefield isn't his favourite player, I know that he knows Real Madrid are much better when Wakefield is on the pitch. On the television, the camera focuses a lot on Kieran Wakefield warming up. He's wearing an orange bib and doing lots of drills. Even though I don't understand what the commentators are saying, I know they're talking about him. My heart beats faster whenever he sprints across the pitch.

"Is it supercharged?" I ask.

Rochy rolls his eyes. "Well, I haven't touched it."

When you switch a television on, the screen crackles and fuzzes and the glass gets buzzy with electricity. It's one of the best things about televisions. I wait until there is another close-up of Kieran Wakefield and then I put my hand against the glass. The tingles shoot through my fingers and spread up my arm. It's just like when you get a shock from touching a real person.

Rochy shakes his head, but I know he doesn't mind really. If he didn't want me to do it he'd just touch the screen before I arrived and steal the electricity. But he always leaves it for me.

"I can't wait!" I say.

"Shhh!"

In the corner of the room, Rochy's mum rolls over and mutters something sleepily. Luckily she doesn't wake up.

Because Spain is a long way from Indonesia, we can only watch matches at about midnight. This is probably because of how long the signal takes to reach us. Rochy tried to explain time zones to me once but I couldn't concentrate because the football was on. We have to watch with the volume turned down really low so that we don't wake up Rochy's mum. It's also why we whisper and why he tells me to shut up a lot.

"What do you reckon the score will be?" I whisper.

"Four–nil. Belmonte will get a hat-trick and Wakefield will score one."

"Remember how good Wakefield was last week," I say.

"I still think Belmonte will score more than Wakefield – he doesn't like being upstaged."

I don't agree with Rochy, but rather than get into an argument that might wake his mum, I split some more of the pumpkin seeds between my teeth. The football has been replaced by adverts for big shiny cars that I don't recognize, and bottled soft drinks that I do.

"What are they saying?" I ask.

Rochy says that because he speaks a little bit of English, he can understand a little bit of Spanish. He says that most languages are pretty much the same.

"They're telling us to go out and buy that car."

"Why?"

"Why what?"

"Why do they want us to buy that car?"

"They want you to buy it because they need to sell it."

"But what's so good about it?"

"It's really spacious. See, you can fit everything in the back – a bicycle, a dog, your shopping, your kids. The joke is that you can fit so much into the car that it's like having a second house. It's a car for people who have a lot of stuff."

Rochy does say some strange things. Why would anyone need two houses? You can only be in one place at a time.

"Can't they just keep it all in their house? Or have less stuff?"

Rochy shrugs. "Maybe, but they wouldn't sell many cars if the advert said that."

Another advert comes on. This one shows a shiny car speeding around a racetrack. There are huge, grey thunderclouds in the sky – just like during monsoon season – and when it starts raining the tyres splash through puddles in slow motion.

"Is this a car for people with less stuff?" I ask.

"I suppose so," Rochy says. "You wouldn't get much in the back of that car."

The car gets faster and faster, and the operatic music gets louder and louder. Rochy gets up to turn the volume down.

"Who is the woman in the passenger seat?" I ask.

"I don't know," Rochy says, sitting down beside me. "No one."

"She looks like a movie star. She's very pretty."

Another advert comes on. It's almost identical to the one before, only the music and the colour of the car are different.

"Is that the same car?" I ask.

"No, this is a different one." Rochy throws a handful of seeds into his mouth and wipes his hand on his shorts.

"Well, who is this one for?"

"People who like to drive fast in the rain."

It sounds like a bad idea to me.

"Is that the same woman who was in the other car?" I ask.

"No, the other one had darker hair."

"So why do all these cars have women in the passenger seats? Do they come with the car?"

Rochy bursts out laughing, spraying seeds everywhere. He clamps a hand over his mouth and rolls around on the floor. His mum moans and turns over in her sleep again.

"What's so funny?" I ask. I can feel my cheeks growing hot. That feeling like I'm bleeding on the inside.

"You," Rochy says. "You're funny." He gives me a

playful nudge and shakes his head. "But I suppose you're right. Maybe it should say: *Woman not included*."

He keeps giggling, trying to catch his breath. On the television, the man and woman sit side by side in the car. The crack down the middle of the screen makes it look as though there is a wall between them. Then the woman leans over, covering her red lips with a hand, and whispers something in the man's ear. The man's mouth turns up at the edges. He flexes his fingers and grips the steering wheel. The woman smiles directly at the camera. Then the car speeds off into the distance.

Some adverts are really weird.

Finally, the football comes back on. The players have finished warming up and the stands are filling with the luckiest people in the world. When they're old they'll be able to say: "I was there the day the greatest player in the world scored a hat-trick against Valencia." But at least I get to watch the game at Rochy's.

Not long before the game starts, Rochy's sisters get home. I turn round when they mumble hello but Rochy just grunts at the television. In the green glow of the screen, his sisters' lips look black, and their skin is a sickly yellow. I notice their arms are covered in scratches as they drop two sacks just inside the door. One of them takes something out of the smaller sack and sits next to her sister on the corner of the mattress. They start to eat.

"Uh-oh, Budi," Rochy says. "This doesn't look good."

I turn round and see the names of Real Madrid players arranged in formation on the screen: Noguerra, Belmonte, Ochoa, Rubio, Tapia, Bello…

"Where is Kieran Wakefield?"

I look at the list of substitutes at the bottom of the screen. Then I turn to Rochy.

"Where is Kieran Wakefield? I don't understand why he isn't in the team – we just watched him warm up."

Rochy shrugs. I suddenly feel a bit sick.

"Why wouldn't he be in the team?"

"Keep your voice down," Rochy says. "I don't know why he's not playing."

"What are the commentators saying?" I whisper, although I think Rochy's family probably wouldn't mind if I started shouting. Kieran Wakefield is currently a missing person!

Rochy leans in closer to the television but eventually sits back and holds out his hands.

"I can't tell what they're saying," he says. "They're talking too fast. Maybe he got injured in the warm-up. Or maybe he got abducted by aliens."

I don't know which would be worse – I just hope it's a mistake. But when the teams walk out onto the pitch, Kieran Wakefield is nowhere to be seen. All I can imagine is Kieran Wakefield being rushed to hospital. Or being abducted by aliens. It would make sense for the aliens to take Kieran Wakefield because he is the best footballer in the world, and football is the most popular sport. If the aliens wanted a new player for their team, he would be the best choice.

But whatever happened, this is terrible news not just for me, but for Kieran Wakefield, Real Madrid and everyone who loves football. The only people who will be pleased are Valencia and their fans, because now they don't have to worry about his ferocious pace and amazing skill.

I worry about what will happen if Kieran Wakefield is injured. Once a boy at work named Bambang was so ill he couldn't work for a week so he got fired. I ask Rochy whether Kieran Wakefield might get fired for not being able to play.

"Of course not," he whispers. "It's pretty much impossible to sack a footballer. If Kieran Wakefield scored an own goal in every game he would still get paid 360,000 euros a week."

I frown at Rochy. Kieran Wakefield does not score own goals. But I'm also relieved. It would seem silly to pay 150 million euros for someone just to sack him.

"How much is 360,000 euros in rupiah?" I whisper.

"A lot."

"And how much is 150 million euros in rupiah?"

"Even more. Now shut up, the game's about to start."

360,000 euros doesn't seem like a lot, considering I get paid about 250,000 rupiah a week. 150 million euros does seem like a lot though, and it makes me wonder how much Real Madrid would pay to sign me.

I'm not that bothered about the game now that Kieran Wakefield isn't playing. I watch a cockroach climb the wall and wonder whether only being interested when Kieran Wakefield plays makes me a glory supporter. I decide that it doesn't.

About five minutes into the game Valencia score. This is a disaster. Real Madrid are title contenders, and Valencia are rubbish. This wouldn't be happening with Kieran Wakefield on the pitch. Luckily, we equalize about fifteen minutes later.

About ten minutes after that there is a power cut.

This happens quite a lot.

Once it happened at the factory and caused a big

problem with the production line. The shoe-cutting machine stopped working and no one could do their job. The foreman was angry because we were all just standing around not doing any work. He said we wouldn't get that day's wages, even though it wasn't our fault. Then the power came back on when Kurniawan had his arm in the shoe-cutter, trying to dislodge the material...

Rochy and I sit in the dark waiting for the power to come back on. We normally wait a while before giving up, even though they never fix power cuts at night. I can hear Rochy's steady breathing and I ask whether he is still awake.

"Uh-huh," he grunts.

"Oh. Okay. Good. Rochy, will Kieran Wakefield still get paid even though he's not playing?"

"Yeah, he'll still get paid. Footballers get paid for doing nothing most of the time."

"That's not true," I say.

"Shhh. Keep your voice down. And it is true."

"It's not," I whisper. "First of all, it wouldn't be possible to play football all the time. You'd get tired after about two hours. Also, the scores would get too high and referees would need calculators, which are rare and expensive.

"Secondly, footballers train a lot but people don't see it because they don't put it on television. I bet you could fill a bucket with the amount Kieran Wakefield sweats every day in training."

"That's disgusting," Rochy says.

"Thirdly, footballers have to play even in winter. Outdoors. Even if it's raining or snowing. In Spain they have cold winters – so cold you can see your breath and puddles turn to ice. Apparently they're even worse in England where Kieran Wakefield is from."

"I know where Kieran Wakefield is from."

"Fourthly, it's not easy being famous. You have to speak to loads of people who ask the same questions after every game when you just want to wash and go to bed."

"I'd love to be famous."

I shake my head but realize Rochy can't see me, so I sigh as well.

"Everyone thinks that until they become famous, and then they realize they can't go anywhere without someone asking for an autograph or taking a picture. Grandma said it was exactly the same for Elvis Presley. Being famous is not as much fun as it looks."

Rochy doesn't argue. We sit in the dark in silence for another ten minutes or so before I decide to leave. I turn my pockets out to make sure I don't get robbed and kick a stone along the deserted streets.

When I get home I collapse onto my mattress. Even though I'm exhausted, I lie awake worrying about what's happened to Kieran Wakefield. I try to tell myself that everything is fine, but all I can see is Kieran Wakefield hurtling into outer space, and Real Madrid's title hopes vanishing with him.

# 11 EXPLANATIONS FOR THE DISAPPEARANCE OF KIERAN WAKEFIELD (FROM MOST TO LEAST LIKELY)

1. He was horribly injured during the warm-up.
2. León Belmonte got jealous and locked him in the changing room.
3. The manager wanted to rest him for the upcoming match against Barcelona.
4. He is secretly a crime-fighting superhero, and duty called.
5. He was abducted by aliens.
6. He ate something that disagreed with him.
7. He had to go back to England for an important occasion.
8. He got lost down one of the corridors in the Bernabéu.
9. He had an argument with the manager.
10. He got stage fright.
11. His boots were faulty.

# ALL SHOOK UP

In the morning I can barely keep my eyes open. Luckily
the machines are really loud so it's impossible to fall
asleep, but every few minutes I feel my head dropping,
and I have to make an effort to concentrate. Apparently
we're behind on a big order, so all the stations are working
at full speed, and the foreman strides along the rows,
telling us to work faster. There is a big damp patch on the
back of his shirt, and every few minutes he takes a
handkerchief from his pocket and wipes his face.

"Come on, Budi, you're slowing down!"

I try to focus on the boot in front of me, but the stitches
seem to blur into one another. I feel light-headed, and the
constant whirr of sewing machines makes me dizzy. When
the foreman next walks along my row I put my hand up.

"What is it, Budi?" he asks. "Why have you stopped? Is there a problem with your machine?"

"*Bapak*, could I please go outside to get some air?"

A bead of sweat trickles down my cheek, and as I look at the foreman his face twists into a smile.

"Of course you can, Budi." I stand up and his face drops into a scowl. "During your break! We haven't got time to play games today. If you're too lazy to do a bit of hard work, then you can easily be replaced."

I sit down because I feel as though my legs are about to give way. A hot, prickly sensation spreads across my neck, as though someone is sewing my skin.

"How long is it until my break, *Bapak*?"

The foreman looks at the clock. "Two hours. And if I see you leave your station before then, don't bother coming back!"

He strides away, but every few minutes he returns and watches me work.

I keep telling myself that I mustn't fall asleep. I remember when a new girl dozed off at her station, and the foreman was so angry that he dragged her out by her hair. But the heat makes everything heavy – my hands, my head, my eyelids. All I want is to rest against the workbench for a long nap...

My head jerks up. I panic. My heart races. The sudden jolt makes my fingers slip and, before I can take my foot off the pedal, the needle slashes into my fingertip. Pain slices through me. I gasp in silent shock. I'm desperate not to cry in front of Rochy, but tears rush to my eyes. Blood seeps across the upper. I try to free it from my machine without drawing any attention but others are already glancing over. Then a shadow falls over my workbench. I don't need to turn around to know who is standing there. A sour, smoky smell gusts over my shoulder.

"What's going on here?" the foreman asks.

I finally dislodge the upper, still attached to my hand, from beneath the needle. The foreman snatches it from me, ripping the stitches out of my fingertip. Fresh blood runs down my finger. At the edge of my teary vision, the colourful material flaps about in the foreman's hand as he inspects it. The boots are the yellow and orange ones that Kieran Wakefield has been wearing this season.

The foreman tosses the upper onto the workbench next to my machine.

"It's ruined," he says.

I nod without turning around.

"This one will have to be thrown away," he says.

I nod again.

"This is unacceptable," he says.

I start to nod, but flinch as I hear the unmistakable swish of the *rotan*.

It's a strange thing, when the *rotan* hits you on the fleshy part of your arm. You don't feel the pain immediately. There's a moment of shock – like being drenched with a bucket of ice-cold water – and then the shock disappears and a stinging, searing pain spreads across your body. The muscle on the back of your arm twitches. Your whole body shivers. And the only thought your brain can process is: *How can something hurt so much and not bleed on the outside?*

It's because of this shock that it takes me a moment to realize I haven't been hit.

"Rochy!" the foreman shouts. "What are you looking at? Why have you stopped working?"

Rochy quickly feeds another piece of material into his sewing machine, wincing hard against the red welt that's rising on the back of his arm.

"As for you, Budi!" the foreman shouts, pulling me round by the shoulder to face him. "Do you know how much these boots sell for? More than two hundred US dollars a pair! You probably don't even know how much money that is, do you?"

He throws his head back, and I get a glimpse of his yellow teeth, his slimy tongue, his endless laughing mouth.

"Now listen to me," he says, suddenly serious, pressing his face close to mine. "You make another mistake like that and you're out of here, understand? You're already behind, and if you don't make today's quota I'm throwing you onto the street."

He straightens up and runs a hand through his greasy hair.

"I'll be watching you," he says.

I turn back to my machine.

And then I hear another swish.

And this one is for me.

My heart surges up into my throat. I feel as though I'm about to be sick. The burning pain shoots around my body with every heartbeat. I scrunch my face against the sting and try to ride it out. You never get used to it – it gets more painful every time. It hurts so much that it feels as though the ground is shaking beneath my feet. Then I hear people scream and realize the ground *is* shaking. I look up and see the lights swinging from the ceiling, showering the workbenches with dust and grit.

"Quiet!" the foreman shouts, shadows dancing across his face. "It's only a tremor! Keep working!"

The tremor is over in an instant. The lights continue to swing, but otherwise it's almost as though it never happened.

The pain in my arm begins to fade, but it leaves behind a dull headache that makes me frown. Before I start on the next upper I tie a piece of thread around my fingertip to stop the bleeding. I suck the blood from the cuts. It looks as though something has bitten me. Something with three razor-sharp teeth.

I can feel the foreman's eyes burning into me from up on the walkway. But I don't look around once.

I work as fast as I can, but it's hard because I have to keep my bloody finger away from the boots so I don't stain them. Every few minutes I have to stop and suck the blood, which makes my mouth taste like a rusty fence.

When the buzzer finally goes at the end of the day I still have three pairs of boots to stitch to meet my quota. Everyone else gets up and shuffles towards the exit. Within minutes I'm the only one left in the room. There is no noise except for the beeping of scooters outside, and the purring of my machine.

I finish stitching the last upper and place it on the pile on the workbench. As I arch my back, the burning feeling in my shoulders gets hotter before fading away. My neck clicks.

A door slams above me, and I spin around to see the foreman twisting a key in his office door. He takes a few steps along the walkway before he notices me.

"Budi," he says, frowning suddenly. "You're still here? Did you fulfil your quota?"

"Yes, *Bapak*."

"Well, what are you waiting for? Go home."

"Yes, *Bapak*."

I walk towards the exit as the lights go out, row by row. At the door I turn back and see the tip of the foreman's cigarette glowing in the darkness.

Rochy is waiting for me outside.

"Sorry I got you caned," I say.

"It's okay, it wasn't your fault."

We compare welts. Rochy's is the colour his Manchester United shirt should be.

"I found out why Wakefield didn't play last night," he says.

My breath catches in my chest.

Here we go.

This is it.

"He injured a muscle in his thigh during the warm-up,

but apparently it's not too serious."

I breathe out and feel my body relax.

"What was the final score?"

"We won four–one. Belmonte scored two goals."

"Cool. When is the next match?"

"Tomorrow. Against Sevilla."

"Will Wakefield be fit enough to play?"

Rochy shrugs. "I don't know. Probably not, but hopefully he'll be back in time for El Clásico next weekend."

El Clásico is when Real Madrid play Barcelona. It's the most important fixture of the season. To lose an El Clásico match would be a disaster.

"I suppose you don't feel like playing a match tonight?" Rochy asks.

I shake my head. "I just want to go home and sleep."

"Me too. I'll see you in the morning."

We go our separate ways, and as I pass the street stalls I wonder what I've got for dinner. Then I remember that it's Friday, and we don't have dinner on a Friday. And definitely not when Dad is still waiting to be paid.

When I get home Grandma is asleep and Dad is still at work. Mum covers the cuts on my fingertip and knee with coconut butter, and while she's not looking I eat a scoop for the bruise on the back of my arm. Then I head to my room.

"You need to be more careful," she calls as I lie down on the mattress.

"I know," I say sleepily. "Everything will be fine when I'm a footballer."

"Coconuts don't grow on trees, you know." I can tell Mum is smiling as she says it.

"Yes, they do."

Mum says something else but I don't catch it, and it's too much effort to ask her to repeat herself. My eyelids droop, but before I fall asleep I notice a small crack in the centre of the ceiling.

I wonder how far away the tremor was felt.

# TROUBLE

When I wake up in the morning I lie on my bed, looking at the crack in the ceiling. It seems to have sprouted mini cracks in the night, the way branches grow from a stem. If there was another tremor then I must have slept through it. I roll over onto my side and rub my eyes. The air coming in through my window feels warm and sticky, and slowly I pull myself up into a sitting position on the side of the mattress. It feels as though I've forgotten something important, and while I sit on the bed, scratching my messy hair, I close my eyes and try to remember.

Then it comes to me in a flash.

I leap off the bed and rush from my room. My parents are already up, sitting at the table, but Grandma is still asleep in her armchair.

"Wake up, Grandma! It's my birthday!"

Her head jerks up, and for a few seconds she just blinks. Then she realizes what's going on and smiles.

"Happy birthday, Budi."

She reaches out and draws me into a big hug.

"Happy birthday, son," Dad says, standing up and ruffling my hair. He's wearing his white shirt and his hair is neatly combed. A folded newspaper is tucked under his arm.

Mum comes over and gives me a hug. "I remember when you were just a baby and I could carry you in one arm. Now look at you – I can hardly believe it."

"You're almost as tall as me," Dad says.

"Quite the young man," says Grandma.

I smile and look at each of them in turn. It feels as though I'm getting taller as I stand here.

"I hope you're hungry," Mum says. "Your father has been out already to buy some fresh fruit and bread."

A big bowl of chopped-up fruit sits in the centre of the table, and Mum brings a bread roll for each of us from the kitchen.

My stomach feels as though it's eating itself, and the sight of so much food makes me rush to my seat. On the table in front of my chair there is a present. It's long and thin and wrapped in old newspaper sheets. As I take my seat I notice that everyone is watching me with big grins on their faces.

"Go on then," Grandma says. "Aren't you going to open it?"

"Shouldn't I wait until after breakfast?"

"Don't be silly," Grandma says. "Presents are for opening, not looking at. That fruit salad isn't going anywhere."

I pick up the gift and try to guess what it might be. It feels very light and is shaped like a tube. I carefully begin to unwrap the present, trying not to rip the newspaper.

"Don't worry about that!" Grandma says. "Tear it open!"

I grab big handfuls of paper, throwing them on the floor around my chair.

"What is it?" I ask, turning the white tube over in my hands.

"Take the rubber band off," Dad says.

I slide the band to the end of the tube and realize that whatever it is must be rolled up.

"Is it a poster?" I ask.

"Have a look and find out for yourself," Mum says. But I can tell from her smile that I've guessed it.

Standing up, I hold the top edge and unroll the glossy paper. First I see a pair of hands together, as if they're clapping. In the background is a blurry crowd. I unravel the poster a little further and see that beneath the hands are white sleeves. I unroll the poster even more and see that Kieran Wakefield is staring back at me.

"This is so cool!"

"Keep going," Mum says.

I keep unravelling the poster and see the brilliant whiteness of his Real Madrid shirt, then his shorts, and finally his socks. Then I see his boots and almost collapse.

"He's wearing my boots! He's wearing the boots that I make at the factory!"

"Keep going," Mum says again. "That's not the best bit."

I unroll the poster to its full length and this time I do collapse into my chair. In the bottom right-hand corner, against the green of the pitch, is Kieran Wakefield's autograph. THE POSTER IS SIGNED BY KIERAN WAKEFIELD HIMSELF! I open my mouth to speak but nothing comes out.

"What's the matter?" Grandma asks. "Turn it around so I can have a look."

I hold it up for Grandma to see. She squints at the poster for a few seconds before nodding her head.

"Very nice," she says. "Although he's nowhere near as handsome as Elvis."

"Do you like it?" Mum asks.

"I love it! It's the best present ever!"

I carefully roll the poster up, put the elastic band round the middle, and take it to my bedroom. Then I give everyone another hug.

"Very good," says Grandma finally. "Now, let's eat."

The fruit salad is delicious, and the bread rolls are warm and soft. Everyone is in a really good mood and at one point Grandma even sings an Elvis song. Dad reads his newspaper and tells us that the pay rise must be just around the corner because the politicians are about to pass a law. Apparently you can't change anything without a law being passed first.

Dad says, "Once the legislation goes through everything should be in place. After that, maybe we'll be able to have fruit salad and fresh bread every morning."

"And I can go to Spain to watch Real Madrid win the league!"

Mum and Dad laugh, but Grandma is too busy cramming orange segments into her mouth to pay attention to anything else.

"Do you want to invite Rochy over for dinner tonight?"

Mum asks. "He's such a nice boy and it's been so long since we last saw him. I'm making extra spicy *rendang* with *martabak* pancakes for dessert."

"Yes, please! Then we can go to his apartment to watch the match."

"Who are they playing tonight?" Dad asks.

"Sevilla, so it should be an easy three points."

Dad wipes his mouth and folds his newspaper up.

"Right, son, we'd better get going or we'll be late for work. And if that happens there'll be no fresh fruit or bread for anyone."

I go to my room and put my shoes on. The poster is lying on the bed, and I quickly unroll it to have one last look.

I can't believe I own a poster signed by Kieran Wakefield.

I run my hand over the autograph in the corner, following the loops and lines of the ink. As I trace my finger over it I can almost hear the crowd chanting his name.

"Come on, birthday boy!" Dad calls from the other room. "We've got to get going."

I roll the poster up and hide it down the side of my bed. The poster is worth a lot of money so I don't want it to get damaged or stolen. Then I rush out to meet Dad, waving goodbye to Mum and Grandma as we leave.

When I get to the factory the foreman is standing behind my seat. Rochy is already at his station, a dark patch of sweat circling the number seven on his back. He doesn't look round.

"Not today, Budi," the foreman says, shaking his head. He raises a hand and points the *rotan* towards the boxing section. "That's where you'll be for the time being. We can't afford any more mistakes like yesterday."

I turn to face the boxing section.

Stacks and stacks of shoeboxes.

Sheets and sheets of wrapping paper.

Roll after roll of sticky labels.

Happy birthday to me.

I spend two hours assembling cardboard boxes, two hours stuffing paper inside boots, and two hours wrapping and boxing boots. Then I have a break. Then I spend another two hours attaching labels to boxes, and two hours stacking boxes onto a trolley and wheeling them into the loading room.

When the buzzer finally goes I've almost forgotten it's my birthday. Rochy meets me by the exit and we walk home in silence. It's only when I smell the *rendang* that I begin to cheer up.

"Hello, Budi," Mum calls from the kitchen. "Hello, Rochy. It's good to see you again. How is your mother?"

"Very well, *Ibu*."

"And your sisters?"

"They're also well, thank you."

Mum smiles and stirs the contents of a pan.

"This won't be ready for a while so you can go out and play if you like."

"It's *training*, Mum, not playing! How many times! Anyway, I've got to show Rochy my poster first."

"Okay," she says. "I'll call you when it's ready."

Rochy says hello to Grandma and then I take him to my room and retrieve the poster from down the side of my bed. I unroll it and place it on my mattress, pinning it down with my hands.

"That's amazing," Rochy says. "Where did your parents find it?"

"I don't know. It must have been really difficult to get hold of. Look at where he's signed it."

Rochy stoops over and squints at the black squiggle in the corner.

"There's a number eleven in that loop," I say. "Can you see? That's how you know it's genuine. Isn't it perfect?"

Rochy straightens up, nodding. "It's really cool."

I gaze at it for a few moments before rolling it up and putting it back in its hiding place.

"Aren't you going to put it up on the wall?" Rochy asks.

"No way! Do you know how much this must be worth?"

"No. Do you?"

"Well, a lot. It's way too valuable to just stick on the wall. What if there's another earth tremor – or a leak in the apartment above – and it gets ruined? Or what if someone sees it through the window and climbs in to steal it?"

"I don't think anyone's going to climb through your window to steal it," Rochy says.

"Well, I don't want to take that chance. You're the only person who knows where I've hidden it, so make sure you don't tell anyone."

"All right, I won't."

"Do you promise?"

"Yes, Budi." Rochy sighs and places a hand over his heart. "I promise not to reveal the whereabouts of your poster to a living soul."

"Good. Now we can go and do some training."

Rochy goes to fetch Fachry, Uston and Widodo while I practise kick-ups in the square. Everything around me –

the dusty streets, the crumbling buildings, the litter – blurs into patches of brown and grey as I loop the ball from one foot to the other. Within a couple of minutes the others have arrived, and we split into two teams.

"You're going down this time!" Uston says as Fachry kicks the ball into the air.

"We'll see!"

I control the ball as it comes down and flick it between Widodo's legs. Rochy shields the ball from Uston and passes it back to me. Widodo lunges in, but I'm too good at dodging tackles and he slides past as I drag the ball back. Fachry tries to narrow the angle but I strike the ball into the top corner.

"One–nil!" Rochy shouts.

I make the shape of a heart and pat my chest where the Real Madrid badge should be.

Uston swears at Widodo and tells him to stay on his feet.

Fachry kicks the ball high into the air for the restart, and it drops perfectly for a volley. Uston rushes to close me down as I swivel my body round and blast the ball as hard as I can. But Uston manages to get his body in the way, and instead of flying towards the goal, the ball rebounds off his back in the opposite direction.

Towards the Dragon's house.

It's like watching a slow-motion replay of a Lazaro Celestino goal. My heart plummets into my stomach. The blood in my veins turns to ice. And I'm completely helpless as the ball flies through a first floor window.

Luckily, the windows round here aren't the type with glass in them, but I hear a smash from inside the room, followed by raised voices.

I stand rooted to the spot. My whole body seems to shudder with every heartbeat. A film of clammy sweat sticks to my forehead.

This is the last birthday I'll ever have.

I look around for something – anything – that might save me. Rochy, Uston and Widodo stand with their mouths open. Fachry is already gone.

Then a voice booms from behind me, and I turn back to the Dragon's house.

"Whose ball is this?" the man asks. It's not the Dragon, but it is one of his brothers. He stands on the top step, holding the ball at arm's length in a big, bejewelled hand. His shirt is open to the heat, exposing his hairy chest and round belly. I try to raise my arm, but the muscles won't respond. Rochy once told me it's impossible to punch yourself in the face. (He was right. I tried it and couldn't do it.) He said your brain stops you from hurting yourself. That's what must be happening to me now. Out of the corner of my eye, I notice Rochy's hand going up.

"It belongs to Budi!" Uston shouts, and I spin around to see him pointing a finger at me. Then he turns and flees down one of the alleys, with Widodo following close behind.

Slowly, I turn back to face the Dragon's brother. He grins at me, showing a set of small, reddish teeth. Whenever I watch a movie at Rochy's, it's never good news when the bad guys smile. It means they've come up with an idea that they like. And more than anything, the Dragon's Clan like making people pay.

"Don't just stand there, little man. Come and get your ball back."

My brain obviously thinks that standing like a statue and disobeying the Dragon's brother is more dangerous than walking towards him, because my feet start to shuffle through the dust in the direction of the apartment block. Rochy begins to follow, but the Dragon's brother scowls and shoos him away.

"If you want to be able to walk home I suggest you get lost now, kid!"

I glance at Rochy and he gives me a weak smile. Then he takes a step back.

As I reach the top step the Dragon's brother puts a hand on my back and steers me into the building. I try to look back at Rochy but the Dragon's brother blocks my view.

"Let's go upstairs and talk about football," he says. "The Dragon is a big fan, you know."

I don't say anything and keep my eyes down. The ground crunches beneath my feet. The stairwell is littered with broken bottles and cigarette butts and bits of tinfoil. And everywhere I look there are these red splats, like blood.

We reach the first floor and turn into a room that's even filthier than the stairwell. And the whole floor is red. Like it's been painted with blood. I can't look at it without thinking about my bleeding problem. I guess it won't be such a problem when I'm dead. In the centre of the room there is a low table with two pairs of feet resting on it. And between them a bottle lies on its side, its neck broken and the golden contents dripping over the edges of the table. A ceiling fan stirs warm air around me, and a sharp smell catches in my throat like petrol.

"This is the kid," the Dragon's brother says. He leaves

me by the door and slumps down into a chair. I keep my eyes down.

"Thank you, Bayu." The voice is unfamiliar, but I know who it belongs to. "So you're a football fan like me, huh?"

I nod without looking up. A murmur of laughter passes round the room.

"It's a good idea to look at me when I'm talking to you."

I raise my head and meet the Dragon's stare. He's frowning and smirking at the same time. But mostly frowning. Two gold chains sit on his chest, and I wonder whether it's the weight of them that makes his breathing shallow and raspy. As he watches me, he twists a ring around one of his thick fingers, smiling properly to reveal a row of crooked, red teeth.

"Hey, I know this kid," says the man sitting beside the Dragon. "I've seen him somewhere before."

As I turn to look at the man he takes his feet off the table and sits forward. I recognize him from the factory. He's the brother that makes collections from the foreman.

"You work at the factory, don't you?"

I nod, because I don't trust my voice to work.

"I knew you looked familiar. What section do you work on?"

"I sew," I say, my voice croaky.

"Sewing?" asks the brother who brought me upstairs. "Isn't that a girl's job?"

He grins. I keep my mouth shut.

"I suppose you get to hang around with girls all day, and that *can't* be bad."

"I don't think girls are that great," I mumble.

They all laugh, even the Dragon. Maybe if I make them laugh enough, they'll give me my football back and let me go without cutting my feet off. The Dragon turns his head to the side and spits a jet of red saliva over his shoulder. That's when I realize it's not blood on the ground – it's spit. They must all chew *sirih*, and that's why their teeth are stained and the floor is covered in red splats.

"Don't worry," the Dragon says. "That will all change soon. Then you'll realize you've got the best job in the world."

He winks, but I shake my head.

"The best job in the world is playing football professionally. That's what I want to do when I'm old enough."

"Ha!" The Dragon scratches his thinning hair. "So you're the next Lazaro Celestino, huh? We could use someone like him in the national squad. We were lucky to beat the Filipinos last month."

The brothers mumble their agreement.

"No," I say. "Not like Lazaro Celestino. Not like Lazaro Celestino at all. I would never play for Barcelona. Barcelona are scum."

"Ah, so you're a Real Madrid man? Belmonte?"

"No, Wakefield."

The Dragon whistles through the gaps in his teeth. "That's one expensive pair of feet. Well, I hope you get there one day, little man. Remind me to raise your rent when you do, yeah?"

They all laugh. I try to smile but can't.

"What happened to your leg?" the Dragon asks.

I look down and see that a trickle of blood has leaked through the crusty layer of coconut butter.

I shrug like it's no big deal. "I injured myself playing football."

"You should be more careful," he says. But the way he says it makes it sound like he doesn't mean it. Then he looks at the broken bottle on the table and raises his eyebrows.

"You'd better go and fetch us a new bottle of whisky," the Dragon says.

I look from one brother to another. "I can't afford one," I mumble.

"What was that?"

"I don't have enough money."

"Well, then I suggest you go and steal one."

"Hang on," Bayu – the brother with my football – says, "I've got a better idea. Boaz, weren't you saying you wanted a pair of football boots for your son's birthday? And that *kurang ajar* foreman wouldn't give you one lousy pair?"

The brother I recognized from the factory nods.

"That's right. He said every pair had to be accounted for, and if one went missing there would be a big problem. I felt like getting my knife out and giving him a big problem right there and then."

"Well," says the Dragon, "here is your solution. Little Lazaro can bring us the boots."

All three brothers turn to look at me. A bead of sweat trickles down the side of my face.

"If you don't want this little incident to cause any trouble for your family," the Dragon says, "I suggest you accept our generous offer and do this favour for Boaz."

"And what if I don't do it?" I ask. "What if I can't?"

The Dragon takes a deep breath, and his big chest swells.

"If you don't do it I'll pay some street rat a few thousand

rupiah to do the job, and then I'll let the foreman know who *I* think the thief might be. Then you'll be on the first boat to Nusa Kambangan."

I look down at my feet and imagine being dragged out of a cell in the middle of the night. Imagine being marched to a quiet spot. "Kneeling or standing?" they ask, and then they pull the trigger. I think of my uncle and shiver.

"Is that a yes?" the Dragon asks.

I nod.

"Good boy. Boaz, tell Little Lazaro what you need."

"It's my son's birthday on Tuesday," he says, "so I need them before then. I don't really care about the colour – I just need a pair to shut my wife up. She's always telling me that our boy should get the best of everything. Blah blah blah. She gives me a headache, you know what I mean?"

I nod again, even though I don't really know what he means. Mum never gives Dad a headache.

"They need to be the type with rubber soles, not studs. And don't you dare bring me a fake pair like the ones you're wearing, understand? I'll be able to tell if you do. I've got the size written down on a piece of paper somewhere."

He starts digging into his pockets, searching through thick wads of cash until he comes across a crumpled bit of paper.

"I made a note for the foreman but he didn't even look at it, the *anjing*."

He stands up and hands the piece of paper to me. Written in shaky handwriting is a line of letters followed by a line of numbers:

| US | UK | EUR | JPN |
|----|----|-----|-----|
| 3  | 2  | 34  | 22  |

"Now," says the Dragon, taking my football from Bayu. "Fetch!"

He hurls it out of the window, and I turn and run as fast as I can. The brothers' laughter echoes after me down the stairwell. I grab my football from the middle of the square and run towards home. As I round the corner, Rochy gets up from the kerb and puts an arm out to stop me. I double over, breathing hard.

"Budi, what happened?"

I can't talk so I pass him the piece of paper. He unfolds the note and frowns at it.

"What's this?"

"My family…" I say. "Have you told my family?"

"What? No. I was going to, but I wanted to speak to you first. What's this about? What happened?"

"They want me to steal for them," I say, straightening up, and the words or the movement make me feel queasy.

"They want you to…" Rochy's voice trails off as he looks at the piece of paper. "They want you to steal from the factory?" he whispers.

"They want a pair of boots with rubber soles by Tuesday," I say, shaking my head.

"In this size?" Rochy asks, but he doesn't wait for my reply. "Budi, you're not going to do it, are you?"

"What choice do I have?"

"But if you get caught you'll never work again! Think about what the foreman would do to you. You can't do it! You've got to go back and beg the Dragon. There must be another way."

"He said if I don't do it he'll use somebody else and frame me. It's no good."

I can tell Rochy knows it's true. We stand together for a few moments, listening to the noises we hear every day: the hum of generators, the clank of pots and pans, the chatter of families, the drone of scooters, the barking of dogs and the shrieking of cats. Only tonight they seem different, like I'm listening to them through a thick wall. Like if I followed one sound in particular I'd never be able to find the source.

"Come on," Rochy says. "Your family are waiting. We've got to try and pretend this never happened."

We both look at the piece of paper and then Rochy rips it into tiny pieces and lets them flutter to the ground.

"Forget about that," he says, smiling. "It's your birthday! Let's eat some *rendang* and watch the greatest team on earth take Sevilla apart!"

I smile, but underneath it there's that feeling like the Dragon's hand is on the knife. Like a spurt of blood just jumped from my heart, and the thick drops are trickling down through me. I try to ignore it.

As we enter the apartment the smell of spices makes my mouth water. I smile. I help Grandma with her tablets and Mum brings the meal over from the kitchen. I keep smiling.

"I don't know if Budi told you," Mum says to Rochy, "but this *rendang* is extra spicy. I hope you don't mind."

"Of course not, *Ibu* – the spicier the better."

"That's what I always say," Grandma says. "It's impossible to have a dish that's *too* spicy. Spice is good for you – the hotter the better."

"Good," Mum says, pouring the curry onto individual trays. "I just hope I've made enough to fill two growing boys."

By the time the first mouthful reaches my stomach, my mouth is on fire. My tongue tingles and my cheeks start to go numb. Dad's forehead is dotted with tiny beads of sweat, and every few minutes he takes a big gulp of water.

"You never could handle your spice, could you, Elvis?" Grandma says.

Dad dabs his forehead and takes another sip from his cup. When he looks up his eyes are watering.

"It's fiery," he says.

Everyone around the table laughs.

"It's very hot," Rochy says, "but it's delicious."

Finally, when we've all finished, the trays are cleared away and Mum brings pancakes to the table. I force myself to eat as many pieces as possible. You never know when you're going to get sweet *martabak* again. When I've finished eating I feel too full to move, and we sit around the table talking for hours. Grandma dozes off and only wakes up when Rochy and I are about to leave.

"What time is the match?" Dad asks. "You don't want to miss it."

"Midnight," I say, standing up from the table. "Come on, Rochy, we should probably get going."

"It's been lovely having you here for dinner," Mum says to Rochy. "You know you're always welcome."

"Yes," says Grandma, "it's nice to see someone with such a healthy appetite."

"Thank you, *Nenek*," Rochy says. "It's been my pleasure. The food was great."

"Will you send our regards to your family?" Mum says.

"Of course, *Ibu*. And thank you again."

"Take care when you walk home tonight, Budi," Mum says.

"He'll be fine," Grandma replies. "You forget how old he is."

Mum nods and smiles. It looks as though she is about to cry, but I don't know why she would.

As Rochy and I walk over to his apartment we see lights on in some of the buildings, which is a good sign because it means his television will probably work. The roads are virtually empty, and we only occasionally hear something rustle among the piles of rubbish, or see a scooter race past the end of the street.

When we reach his apartment, Rochy's mum is sitting on the mattress in the corner of the room. A table lamp throws a cone of weak yellow light around her, but it's too gloomy to see what she's doing. It looks as though she might be taking some tablets, like Grandma does.

"I've brought Budi round to watch the football," Rochy says. "It's his birthday today."

Rochy's mum grunts but doesn't look up. "Make sure you keep the noise down," she says.

Rochy shakes his head. "Budi's family send their regards."

This time his mum doesn't even grunt.

Rochy turns the television on and we sit cross-legged on the floor. It's a relief to see that Kieran Wakefield has recovered from his injury, and when there's a close-up I reach forward and touch my hand to the screen. The shock shoots up my fingers and makes my arm tingle. Then the camera focuses on León Belmonte, who is sitting in the stands wearing a suit and sparkly earrings and a watch.

"Why isn't Belmonte playing?" I ask.

Rochy shrugs. "Maybe they want to rest him for El Clásico next weekend. It looks like it's all up to Wakefield tonight."

The football programme is replaced by an advert for beer. Then that advert is replaced by a different advert for a different beer. Then that advert is replaced by a different advert for a different beer. I start to feel really thirsty.

"Rochy, why are there so many types of beer?"

Rochy shrugs. "Maybe they all taste different."

"I didn't realize that drinking beer made you so popular."

"What do you mean?"

"Well, everyone in these adverts has loads of friends."

"They're not real people," Rochy says. "They're actors. In real life, the more beer you drink, the fewer friends you have. You know that man who sleeps in one of the big bins at the factory during the rainy season?"

"Yeah."

"He drinks a lot of beer, and I've never seen him with any friends."

"That's because he smells."

"No, he smells because he lives in a bin, and he lives in a bin because he drinks a lot of beer. You can't pay rent if all your money goes on beer, and you can't keep a job if you're always drunk."

"So why does he drink a lot of beer if it means he has to live in a bin?" I ask. "Why doesn't he just drink water or something else instead?"

"Because beer is addictive. When you drink beer you feel happy for a while, but then you fall asleep and wake

**101**

up with a headache. Sometimes you're sick and can't remember anything. The more beer you drink, the more beer you *have* to drink. That man who lives in the bin has got to the point where he needs to drink beer just to feel normal. It's sad really."

"So why does beer look so good on television?"

Rochy sighs. "Everything looks good on television. It's hard to explain."

"Try," I say. "Please."

Rochy pauses for a moment, then shuffles round to face me properly.

"Okay," he says. "Imagine you want me to buy something from you."

"Like a pair of football boots?"

"Right, like football boots. If you tell me they're the best boots ever – that they'll make me a World Cup winner – I'll want to own a pair. If I see someone like Kieran Wakefield wearing them, I'll want a pair even more. That's why footballers get paid so much money to play in particular boots – it makes thousands of people want those boots for themselves."

"So it's kind of like a bribe?"

"Yes, like a bribe. Everyone on television is being bribed to make you want things. Do you understand?"

I frown. A cockroach crawls out of the shadows and scurries back again. "I think so."

Rochy looks down at his legs and picks at a small scab on his knee.

"If you understand that," he says, turning back to the television, "then you understand a lot."

The football programme comes back on, and the floor in front of the television is bathed in green light. As the teams line up before kick-off, Rochy's sisters arrive home. I hear the scrape of their flip-flops long before they walk through the doorway. When I turn round and say hello they just drop their sacks and grunt. I wonder if they realize they're becoming like their mum. Then they kick off their flip-flops, walk straight across the room, and collapse onto the bed next to her. I look at Rochy but he doesn't seem to notice.

As much as I try to enjoy the football, every time there is a close-up of someone's boots I'm reminded of the Dragon's demand. It doesn't matter who the player is, or what kind of boots he's wearing; I just can't help thinking about what I have to do. I know something is really wrong when Kieran Wakefield scores a header and I don't even feel like celebrating.

I'm almost glad when there's a power cut midway

through the second half. I don't wait to see whether it will be fixed. I just get up, turn my pockets out, and start heading back.

When I get home I go straight to my room and fall onto my mattress. I stare up at the ceiling. It feels like a long time since I noticed the new cracks.

I roll over and reach down the side of my bed for the poster. There is just enough moonlight for me to see the autograph in the corner, and I trace the lines over and over with my fingertip.

My eyes begin to close, and I roll the poster up and return it to its hiding place.

But not before I kiss the feet that are wearing my boots.

# ONLY BELIEVE

The next day is Sunday, so the factory is closed and everybody gets a day off. I wake up early with a watery feeling in my stomach. It's still dark, but no matter how many times I toss and turn I can't get back to sleep. So I decide to get up and head to the latrine round the back of the block.

Normally there is a queue to use the toilet in the morning, but if you get up early enough on a Sunday you can walk straight in. I lock the door, drop my shorts and squat over the hole. The little shed is always like an oven, even early in the morning, and the smell is sharp enough to make you stop breathing. Tiny insects crowd around the dim bulb overhead. But it's quiet, and as I squat I have plenty of time to think.

I know that, despite Rochy's warnings, I've got no choice but to steal the boots. The only question is how I should go about it.

Once I saw a film at Rochy's called *The Heist Bandits*. It was about this team of thieves who tried to rob a bank. The first thing they did was draw a floor plan of the building and mark out its weaknesses. Admittedly they did it on a computer, not in the dust of a toilet floor, but I don't know anyone with a computer that makes maps. Or anyone with a computer at all.

I pick up a chunk of wood that's fallen from the door frame and trace an outline of the factory in the dust between my feet. I draw crosses for doors and lines to show where the rows of workstations are. Then I draw a stick figure with an angry face outside the foreman's office.

After the shoes have been boxed, they are stacked up on a trolley and wheeled into a high, dusty area at the back of the factory, ready to be loaded onto a container truck. The room is full of wooden pallets and tall rolls of plastic for wrapping the shoebox towers, so it's perfect for hiding in. The problem is that you always need an escape plan, and the only way out is through a big shutter that needs two men to haul it open using the chains on either side. And even if I could get through it, the fenced compound beyond is always locked.

My only option would be to steal the boots, cross the factory floor, and leave through the staff exit at the front. This would arouse suspicion. And if there's one thing I learned from *The Heist Bandits* (other than how to draw maps and that you always need an escape plan), it's that you don't want to arouse suspicion. When the robbers aroused suspicion in the film, most of them ended up being killed. Obviously I want to avoid making the same mistakes.

My only hope is that I'll be able to use the confusion of everyone leaving at the end of the day to slip into the loading room. Then, when I've got the boots, sneak out while the foreman is in his office.

Looking at the map for a final time, I scuff it with my feet to destroy the evidence and head back to the apartment. As I come through the door I hear Grandma coughing quietly, but it's so dark that I can't tell whether she is asleep or not. Her head is slumped forward onto her chest, but as I shake her arm she jolts upright and lets out a little cry.

"Who is it?" she asks. "Who's there?"

"It's okay, Grandma," I whisper. "It's me, Budi. Are you all right?"

"Oh, yes, dear. You just gave me a bit of a shock. What's the matter?"

"I can't sleep," I say, sitting on the rug next to her feet. In the dark I hear Grandma fumbling with something in her lap, and a few moments later a match throws white light onto everything. Grandma lifts the flame to a cigarette between her lips and shakes the match out, dropping it into the ashtray on the arm of her chair. The tip of her cigarette glows in the darkness and, when she takes a drag, her face appears in an orange light before disappearing again.

"Grandma, will you tell me a story, please?"

"Of course," she says in a low voice. "What kind of story would you like?"

"Hmm… How about one where someone gets into trouble but gets out of it again?"

Grandma's orange face appears again, and she looks at me in a strange way.

"Okay, I think I have just the story. Are you sitting comfortably?"

"Yes."

"Then I'll begin. There once was a boy who lived on one of the many islands of Indonesia. It was only a small island, but it was home to one of the biggest palm trees ever known. For some reason this tree had kept growing and growing, high above all the others, and its leaves stood many metres above the canopy. The fishermen used to remark on its height from their boats out at sea."

Grandma pauses, and for a few seconds her face appears in the light of the cigarette. I smell the smokiness of her breath as she exhales.

"The people believed that a giant used to inhabit the island in ancient times, and this was the tree from which he ate. It was thought that anyone who could pluck a coconut from the top of the trunk would receive great health and strength. This didn't work with the coconuts that fell from the tree; they lost all their power upon hitting the sand.

"Now, the children of the island, as you might well imagine, were very fond of this legend. They were also quite adept at climbing palm trees. They used to wrap a rag around the base, straddle the trunk, and shimmy up in no time. However, in all the history of the island, no one had ever climbed this magnificent tree. Most thought it was simply impossible. Many had tried, of course, but as soon as they passed the tops of the other trees they would lose their nerve and climb down. They knew all too well that anyone who fell from such a height would certainly be killed. This is where the boy I mentioned at the beginning comes into it."

Grandma takes another drag, and even after her face disappears I keep staring at the blackness that replaces it.

"One day, when all the fishermen were out in their boats, the boy decided to attempt the climb. His friends had been challenging him all morning, and finally he gave in and agreed to do it. At first his friends shouted lots of encouragement, but as the boy climbed higher and higher they fell silent in amazement. The boy himself was terrified, and as he moved above the other trees the trunk began to sway dangerously. But he faced his fears, kept climbing, and eventually reached the top. All of his friends clapped and cheered, and they shouted at him to climb down. But the boy was too frightened and refused to budge.

"By this time many of the villagers had been drawn to the scene by all the noise, but no one could think of a way to get the boy down. They could hardly climb up and fetch him, could they? If he jumped the fall would kill him, and to cut down such a majestic tree was unthinkable. Eventually, someone suggested calling the fishermen in; they could tie their fishing nets between the tree trunks to make a safety net.

"So that is what they did. The villagers created a net and angled it towards the sea, so that when the boy bounced he would land safely in the water.

"However, the boy still did not want to let go of the trunk. The sun was starting to set, and the villagers began to worry that the boy would stay up there overnight, and if he became exhausted he would fall from the tree and miss the net altogether.

"Then the boy's best friend had a brilliant idea. He told everyone to be quiet and called up to the boy."

Grandma takes a final drag and crushes the cigarette in the ashtray beside her.

"What did he say?" I ask.

"He said: 'You have to pick one of the coconuts and break it open against the trunk. The water will give you special powers. Even if you miss the net, the fall won't harm you.' So the boy, clinging on tightly with his legs and one arm, reached out and picked a coconut. He began hitting it against the trunk, and all the villagers below ran for cover as it started raining coconuts – a coconut falling from that height is a very dangerous thing. Only the boy's best friend remained, and he stood beneath the net as all the coconuts landed harmlessly around him.

"Finally, the boy managed to split the coconut. He lifted it above his face and let the trickle of water fall into his mouth. And do you know something? It was the most delicious coconut he had ever tasted. The water was sweet and flavoursome and refreshing. When he had finished the last drop he felt strong and fearless like a giant. From far below he heard his best friend calling up to him: 'You can do it! You can fly!'"

"But, Grandma, surely that was just a myth. The coconut didn't really give him special powers, did it?"

"Well, listen to the end of the story and you can decide for yourself. The boy looked down from his perch and saw his friend waiting below the net. Suddenly it didn't seem like such a long way down. Still holding onto the coconut, the boy got himself into a crouching position among the leaves. For the first time he actually looked around, and he was amazed by what he could see. There were islands in the distance that he hadn't even heard of, and the ocean stretched away to the horizon in every direction. Everything seemed so quiet, and he was able to think very clearly. Then he took a deep breath and leaped into the air."

Grandma stops talking, and I hear her slow breathing in the darkness.

"Then what happened?" I ask, struggling to control my voice.

"The boy plummeted down and landed in the centre of the net, which catapulted him over the beach and into the warm waters beyond. When he resurfaced, he held the coconut high above his head and all the islanders rushed onto the beach, shouting and cheering. So you see, his best friend was right – he *could* fly."

"That's not flying, Grandma. He just fell out of a tree and got a lucky bounce."

"Don't be so sure, Budi. The coconut did give him a special power: belief. Without belief he would never have been able to jump from the tree. Before you achieve something, you have to believe that you can do it."

Grandma coughs quietly, like a low growl. I get up and feel my way to the kitchen to fetch a cup of water.

"Thank you, dear," she says, after she's taken a sip. "So, did you enjoy your story?"

I coil the rug tassels around my finger while I think about it.

"Yes, Grandma, but I won't be climbing any trees from now on."

"No, you *must* climb trees. The taller the better. If no one took any risks everyone would be doing the same thing for ever. And how boring would that be? Besides, the boy reached the top and got down safely."

"But only because of his friend."

"*Exactly!* Sometimes you have to rely on the ones you love to help you out of a sticky situation. Without his best friend, that boy might still be clinging on for dear life to this day."

"I still think Mum wouldn't be very happy if she found out I'd been stuck up a tree all day."

"That's true," Grandma says, chuckle-coughing, "she would worry. But you mustn't be afraid of making mistakes. It's good to make mistakes. If the boy hadn't got stuck at the top of the tree he would never have become aware of all those other islands beyond his own. Climbing that tree, although it was terrifying, opened his eyes to the world around him. He realized that his own island was part of an archipelago – that's what we call a group of islands – and that this archipelago was probably a small part of a much larger community. And do you know what? He was right. Indonesia is made up of thousands of islands – some say as many as 17,000 – and before he climbed that tree he only knew about his own. Can you guess what he did when he grew up?"

"No, Grandma, what did he do?"

"He repaired one of the old fishing boats that had been damaged in a storm and set off with his best friend to explore the other islands. Some of them were very small and uninhabited – so small you could run a lap of the beach in just a couple of minutes. Others were much bigger and home to unfamiliar plants and animals. Some of them were similar to his own island, except for little differences. And of course, none of them had a palm tree as tall as the one he had climbed as a boy.

"Every so often he would return to his own village and tell the people about his discoveries. To them he was a hero – they welcomed his return with feasts and dancing. And all because once upon a time he had been too scared to move."

We sit silently in the dark for a few moments. Outside, a cat howls.

"Grandma, is that a true story?"

"Of course it is. Do you think I just make these things up on the spot? I've lived for a long time, you know, and I've heard a great many tales. That story is far from being the strangest."

"Will you tell me another one?"

"Maybe in the morning. It's still night-time, and I need my beauty sleep. Sweet dreams, Budi."

"Goodnight, Grandma."

I kiss Grandma on the cheek and go back to my room. I don't feel tired, but the next time I open my eyes the room is light, and Mum is calling me for breakfast.

# ALWAYS ON MY MIND

On Monday morning I spend so long in the latrine that the people outside bang on the door and threaten to knock it down. As much as I'd like to, I can't hide in here for the rest of my life. And the people outside know it. I quickly fasten my shorts and rush out, hoping they'll all be too desperate to chase after me, but one woman manages to clip me on the back of the head as I pass.

The walk to the factory is over too soon, and the morning is so humid that I arrive drenched in sweat. As I approach my station there is someone already sitting next to Rochy.

"Budi!" the foreman calls from the walkway. He points his *rotan* towards the other end of the factory. "Boxing section!"

117

I shuffle between the rows of sewing machines, my stomach a big sack of water. Maybe the worst thing about the boxing section is that you don't have to think at all, so whatever is on your mind just keeps going round and round.

I start assembling shoeboxes, wondering all the time whether I'll be able to carry out my plan. I wonder the same thing while I'm stuffing paper inside boots and wrapping boots in paper. I wonder the same thing while I'm putting boots in boxes and stacking boxes onto trolleys. And every so often I find myself looking towards the doors of the loading bay, knowing that beyond them is where I'll become a thief, just like my uncle. Maybe it runs in the family.

I don't know much about my uncle. I know he did some bad things a long time ago and has been locked up on Nusa Kambangan ever since. But my family never talk about him. He might have been dragged out of his cell and given the choice of standing or kneeling years ago, but I wouldn't know. I think it's because they're ashamed, and the thought of being disowned by my own family makes me bleed a little bit on the inside.

The buzzer goes for the end of the shift and I blink the tears away.

"Come on, Budi," the foreman says, "hurry up and get those shoes in the loading room. Tomorrow I want you back on sewing. The new girl is falling behind."

"Yes, *Bapak*."

Everyone shuffles towards the exit, and I push the last trolley into the loading room. I quickly glance over my shoulder to check I'm alone and start looking for a pair of boots in the right size. There are so many boxes – and so many numbers on each box – that I'm confused at first. Then I spot what I'm looking for. I open the box but the boots inside are studded. I see another pair but they're right at the bottom of a tall stack, and the last thing I need is to topple boxes everywhere and draw attention to myself. Finally, I find a pair in the right size near the top of a stack. I reach up and take the box down. I flip the lid open. Inside is a pair of lime green boots with rubber soles. They're not the type that Kieran Wakefield wears, but they're still cool. I take one out and hold it in my hand, asking myself whether I can really go through with this.

"What are you doing, Budi?"

My heart stops beating. Images of dark cells and mean criminals and rough hands dragging me from my bed in the dead of night flash through my mind.

What will Mum and Dad say?

What will Grandma think?

My heart beats at three times the normal speed.

I feel dizzy.

I feel sick.

I turn around.

Rochy stands in front of the swinging doors, his arms hanging by his sides.

"I think you should put those back," he says calmly.

I nod, placing the boot in the box and returning it to the stack.

"Let's get out of here," Rochy says, "before someone finds us."

I follow him, keeping to the shadows under the walkway, relieved and disappointed at the same time. I might not be going to prison for stealing, but it won't be long until the Dragon sends me there anyway. I had one chance to get the boots for his brother. One chance. And I blew it. By tomorrow morning – maybe even tonight – the Dragon's Clan will realize that I've failed them. And then they'll make me pay.

We get to the end of the walkway and Rochy comes to a stop. He turns and puts a finger to his lips. Above us, the office door slams. The walkway creaks under the weight of someone standing on it. Keys jingle as they're turned in a lock. Then footsteps echo across the empty factory as the foreman makes his way towards the stairs.

"Quick," Rochy whispers. "Under here!"

We scurry to the nearest workbench and crawl under it. I clamp a hand over my mouth to quieten my breathing. The foreman reaches the bottom of the stairs and starts flicking the light switches.

"When the last light goes out," Rochy whispers, "we'll make a run for the door, okay?"

I nod and look at the exit. The door stands ajar, letting in all the sounds from the street outside.

"You go first," he says. "I'll follow."

The room grows darker and darker as each row of lights is turned off. When the final switch is hit, I scramble out from under the workbench. Almost immediately I hear the foreman swear and the electric lights flicker back into life.

I dive under the next workbench, unsure whether the foreman has spotted me. The lights stop flickering, and from my new hiding place I can only see him from the chest down. He stands by the light switches for a moment, his hand hovering over the panel. Then he strides towards me. Within two seconds I can only see him from the belt down. Then the knees down. I back away into the furthest corner, and then only his shoes are visible. I expect an oily hand to reach under the bench and grab me at any moment, but instead a bunch of keys drops onto the surface above me, and the foreman turns around and heads towards the toilet beneath the walkway.

As soon as the door closes behind him, I hear Rochy's voice in an urgent whisper.

"Go!"

I crawl out and make a dash for the exit. Bursting onto the street, I weave through the traffic, not stopping or looking back until I reach an alleyway on the other side of the road.

"That was close," I say.

I turn around, expecting Rochy to be right behind me. But he's nowhere to be seen. The air above the traffic is hazy, blurring my view of the factory door. I look down the street to see if he ran a different way. But there's no sign of him.

"Come on, Rochy, where are you?"

I crane my neck to get a better look at the factory door.

"Come on…"

Then I glimpse the dusty pink of his Manchester United shirt as he emerges from the factory. He zigzags through the traffic and I wave him over to my hiding spot. He's barely made it to safety when the foreman steps out onto the street and locks the door behind him.

"What happened?" I ask.

"Never mind that! What were you thinking? I thought I told you not to take the boots? You could have ruined everything!"

When I look at Rochy I can't stop the tears from rising. I'm bleeding on the inside too, I just know it. I hate crying in front of Rochy. I look at the ground so he won't notice.

"I'm sorry," I say. "I don't know whether I would have taken them or not. I don't know what I was going to do."

Rochy sighs. "Why don't you just go home? I'm sure it's not as bad as you think."

Two tears drop onto the dusty floor of the alleyway. "Okay," I say, not looking up. "I'll see you in the morning."

We go our separate ways, and as soon as I round the corner I break into a run and don't stop until I reach home. It feels as though the faster I run the further away the tears get, the quicker the wound inside heals.

As I turn into the apartment I almost collide with someone coming out.

"Budi!" Mum says, stepping round the man in our

doorway and putting her hands on my shoulders. "You must watch where you're going. Sorry, Doctor, this is our son."

The doctor holds a black briefcase in his hand and wears a shiny watch on his wrist. He glances at me and smiles in an annoyed kind of way, like he's got indigestion. Straightening his glasses on his nose, he quickly checks his watch.

"No need to apologize," he says to Mum. "I'd better be off now."

"Of course," Mum says, rubbing my shoulders. "Thank you for coming at such short notice."

The doctor nods and steps out into the street. Mum lets go of my shoulders with a sigh and rubs her face.

"Honestly," Grandma says, "I don't know why you called a doctor. I'm fine."

When I turn to face Grandma she is fumbling with a packet of cigarettes. She puts one between her lips and I strike a match for her.

"Thank you, Budi," she says, taking a drag.

"Are you ill, Grandma?" I ask.

"No, of course not," she says. "I've never felt better."

"I thought you were going to…" Mum says, wringing her hands. "You wouldn't stop coughing!"

"It was just a coughing fit," Grandma says. "I have them all the time."

"They're not normally as bad as that. You couldn't breathe."

"But I'm fine now, aren't I? So let's just forget about it. You're worrying Budi."

Mum puts her hands on her hips and shakes her head. Grandma exhales a long cloud of smoke.

"The doctor said you should give up smoking," Mum says.

"Doctors say a lot of things."

"You need stronger medication as well. I don't know how we'll pay for that."

"We'll manage," says Grandma, tapping her cigarette on the edge of the ashtray. "We always do."

At that moment Dad walks in, and Mum explains exactly what happened. Meanwhile, Grandma smokes another cigarette, shaking her head the whole time.

"You're blowing things out of proportion," Grandma says, when Mum has finished. "It's really not that bad."

Dad looks concerned but suggests we talk about something else over dinner. No one can think of anything else to talk about so we eat in silence. It's a horrible atmosphere. It's like they know everything that's going on and they're ashamed of me. And no matter what Grandma says, I can tell Mum is really worried. I think about reminding her that Grandma is immune to venom, but change my mind.

Mum gets up to make tea for everybody. Dad tells me about how great everything is going to be when we get the pay rise. He says we'll be able to afford everything we need: food, clothes, medicine.

"I was going to use the extra money to visit the Bernabéu," I say, "but if Grandma needs more medicine she can have it instead."

Mum sighs and shakes her head as she pours out the tea.

"That's very sweet of you," Grandma says. "But I'm sure it won't be necessary."

Mum brings the tea to the table.

"Why don't you go and see if your friends want to play?" she asks.

She doesn't mean play. She means train. She just doesn't know the difference.

I remember how Uston betrayed me, how everyone but Rochy abandoned me to the Dragon's Clan.

"We've fallen out."

"Not to worry, son," Dad says, sipping his tea. "I'm sure you'll be friends again soon."

I don't think I'll be friends with anyone when I'm chained up in some dungeon on Execution Island.

Dad takes another sip from his cup and looks at me through the steam. Then he exchanges a glance with Mum, and she turns to face me.

"Budi, when your father gets the pay rise there's a chance we might be able to afford to send you back to school. How would you feel about that?"

"Do you mean a football academy?"

"No," Dad says, "just a normal school."

I lift my cup to my mouth and take a long sip to give myself more time to think. I try to imagine there isn't a police jeep on its way to arrest me. How would I feel about going back to school? It seems like such a long time since I went there that it's difficult to remember what it was like.

"Would Rochy be able to come too?" I ask.

Dad shakes his head. "I don't think so, Budi, but you'd still be able to see him in the evenings. Plus you'd make lots of new friends."

A vague memory comes back to me. Lots of children sit behind desks, listening to a stern man giving out instructions. A bit like the foreman at the factory, really. Only with better-smelling breath. I suddenly remember being asked to stand up in class and answer a question. But I didn't understand. The other children started snickering, and eventually the teacher ordered me to stand in the corner, facing the wall. Even after he told the class to stop laughing I felt like everyone was watching me.

It feels as though a lump of ice has formed in my throat, and I take another gulp of tea to try and dislodge it.

"I'm not sure," I say. "What if I don't like school?"

"What's not to like?" asks Dad.

"Well, I don't know anything. All the other kids will think I'm stupid."

"No, they won't," Mum says, putting her hand on my arm. "And it doesn't matter if there are things you don't know – that's why you go to school, to learn."

"I wouldn't know anybody," I say, feeling hot. "Anyway, I like working in the factory."

Sometimes, you have to lie a little bit, even to your parents.

"But with an education you could do whatever you want to do," says Dad. "There are so many opportunities. You could become a lawyer."

"A lawyer?" I ask.

"Yes, if that's what you want."

"But it's not what I want. I want to become a footballer. And you don't need to go to school to become a footballer. Rochy says most footballers don't have two brain cells to rub together."

Dad sighs and finishes his tea. "Well, if we can afford it you'll be going to school. And you'll thank me for it one day."

I pull a face but know better than to argue. Instead I look over at Grandma. She's already dozed off in her chair.

"Is Grandma all right?" I ask.

"Of course," says Mum. "She just gave me a bit of a scare today, that's all."

I look into my cup and finish the rest of my tea.

"I think I'll go to bed," I say. "Thanks for dinner, Mum."

Mum and Dad smile, but they look tired. For the first time I realize how old they must be.

I lie awake for what feels like hours. Outside the generators seem louder than usual, and even when they cut out I still can't sleep. Someone races around the streets on a scooter. Two dogs bark at the sound of the engine.

I start to imagine that the dogs are police dogs, coming to drag me away. I wish Grandma was awake, because I could really do with hearing one of her stories.

In the next room, Mum and Dad talk for a long time. I know they're talking about Grandma, even though I can't tell what they're saying.

A single tear rolls from the corner of my eye and pools in my ear, wet and uncomfortable.

I hope Grandma is really asleep, and not just pretending.

# SUSPICIOUS MINDS

When I wake up in my own bed it's almost worse than the alternative – waking up in a prison cell. By now the Dragon and his brothers will have realized I've broken my side of the deal, and it's only a matter of time before they frame me. I wonder when they'll come for me. I wonder who will come for me. Will it be the police? Will they let the foreman punish me first? Will it be the Dragon himself? I stare up at the crack in the ceiling. It seems to reach a little further every time I look at it.

The heat when I step onto the street is overpowering. Even the shady backstreets are hot and airless. It's got to rain soon. I pass a stall selling coconuts and stop to buy some milk. I imagine that the coconut was picked from the giant tree on that faraway island Grandma told me about, and I start to feel stronger with every sip.

But then I turn the corner, and the factory comes into view, and I realize something is horribly wrong. There is a crowd outside the factory, and as I get closer I notice the doors are locked.

The factory doors are never locked at this time in the morning.

Standing in front of the crowd on an upturned plastic crate is the foreman. My stomach squirms as though the coconut milk has gone sour. I shuffle between the scooters and cars in the traffic jam and join the back of the crowd.

A cigarette hangs from the foreman's mouth, and he looks down on us through the smoke as more and more workers join the crowd. I spot *BELMONTE* on the back of Rochy's Manchester United shirt and make my way over to him. He is so busy rolling a stone beneath his foot that he doesn't notice me at first.

"Hi, Rochy. How's it going?"

As he looks up I see how tired he is.

"Oh, not bad."

"Do you know what's going on?" I ask.

He shakes his head. "No idea. They're not letting anyone in for some reason."

I imagine the foreman announcing that there is someone at the factory who thinks it's acceptable to steal. Everyone looks around at one another, tutting and shaking their heads. Then I imagine the foreman calling someone out of the factory to identify the thief. It's the Dragon. Even though I try to hide, he still manages to point me out, and I get dragged in front of everyone and humiliated.

I try to think of something else. Rochy is rolling the stone again, looking down.

"What did you get up to last night?" I ask.

"Huh? Nothing. You?"

"Not much." For some reason I don't feel like telling him about Grandma. "My parents want to send me to school when we get the pay rise."

"Lucky you."

Rochy looks at his feet the whole time. More workers press in behind us, so that if I wanted to escape I would have to push through a wall of bodies. The air smells of sweat and soil and petrol. I watch the foreman's face over the shoulder of the person in front, and he takes one last look around before spitting his cigarette onto the ground.

"Quiet, all of you! Listen up!"

Everyone stops talking, but the foreman still has to shout over the traffic.

"Most of you are probably wondering why I've gathered you out here this morning, although at least one person knows the reason why!"

The foreman pauses and squints into the crowd. The sun seems to get hotter with each passing second, and I can feel the sweat trickling across my scalp. Rochy watches the foreman, but his foot keeps dragging the stone from side to side.

"It displeases me to announce that we have a thief in our midst!"

For a moment it feels as though the coconut milk is about to surge up into my mouth, but I clamp my lips together and swallow as hard as I can. The workers around me start murmuring, and their bodies press closer against my skin.

"Quiet! Last night somebody broke into the factory and stole a pair of boots! The police have been informed, but it will be a lot better for the perpetrator if he or she comes forward now and confesses!"

Everyone shuffles and looks around at one another. Rochy lifts his foot and stares at the round stone beneath. There is a deep groove in the dirt where it has been rolled from side to side. The Dragon must have already sent someone to steal the boots, which means it won't be long until I become the prime suspect. The crowd presses in. Someone's hairy arm, slick with sweat, slides across my neck as they jostle for space.

"I know this was an inside job, and if anyone is found to be withholding information they will be punished just as severely as the thief. In the meantime, everyone will suffer as a result! Does anyone have anything they wish to say?"

The foreman stares into the crowd, and for a second our eyes meet. Then he steps down from his box and turns towards the factory.

"Very well," he says, "but you have been warned!"

The foreman punishes us by making everyone work on unfamiliar sections. Me and Rochy get put on boxing. Sometimes it feels as though I spend my whole life boxing boots.

The foreman paces along the row saying: "You'll work on this section for as long as it takes to find the thief. And if we're behind at the end of the day you'll go back to your stations and keep working until the orders have been met. Are you sure you don't know anything about what happened? You know my office door is always open if you want to have a chat. In the meantime, I suppose I'll just suspend everybody's pay. Maybe that will help you to remember."

This is bad news. If our pay is suspended it means we might never get paid again. And if we never get paid again, we won't receive the pay rise and I won't be able to pay for Grandma's medication and I definitely won't be able to save enough money to go to the Bernabéu.

After about an hour of pacing around each section, the foreman goes up to his office and closes the door.

"Rochy," I whisper. "Do you think the Dragon hired someone to steal the boots?"

Rochy frowns and shakes his head. "I don't know," he says, wrapping a pair of boots in paper and putting them in a box. "Maybe." Another pair goes in another box. "But we really shouldn't be talking." And another pair. "The boss is really angry." And another. "He's looking for any excuse to get rid of people." And another. "So leave me alone."

The foreman reappears on the walkway and places one hand on the railing. In the other he holds up a wad of cash.

"Listen up, all of you! I'm offering a reward to anyone who comes forward with information about the thief – a one-off cash sum!" He waves the money. "And you don't need to worry about being viewed as a confederate – I'm willing to overlook the fact you may have been concealing information. Come and see me whenever you like. Now, get back to work!"

Everyone in the factory seems to be whispering all of a sudden, but Rochy looks like he's in a trance.

"Psst!" I say. "Did you hear that? A one-off cash sum. Like the lottery. How much money do you reckon he was holding?"

"I don't know," Rochy says. "What does it matter?"

"Well, if we knew who stole the boots that money could be ours."

"But we don't know who stole the boots," he says.

"I know, but we could try and work it out. We know the Dragon must have hired someone so we've already got a lead. And if we find out who he hired I'll be off the hook. *And* the reward might be big enough to cover Grandma's medication and a trip to Madrid."

Rochy opens his mouth as if to say something, but instead he just huffs and goes back to boxing shoes.

"We could make it fun – like being detectives. Do you remember that television show we watched? You could be my sidekick."

"No, Budi—"

"Okay, okay. I'll be the sidekick, but I still get to carry a gun and drive the car. First, we have to start looking for clues. We also need to find out whether there were any witnesses—"

"Forget about it, Budi. The Dragon wouldn't be stupid enough to leave any clues. The whole idea's stupid. Just forget about it."

I shove a pair of boots into a box and chuck them on top of the pile.

"Why are you being so stubborn?" I ask. "And why won't you help me?"

Rochy pretends not to hear me. I ram another pair of boots into a box.

During my lunch break I go to the canteen and try to think of ways to solve the mystery over a tray of rice and "Sauce of the Day". At the table next to me a couple of women have a whispered argument, which makes it hard to concentrate. Thankfully they soon get up and leave, but I begin to realize that catching the thief might be harder than I thought.

These things are so much easier to solve on television.

The buzzer goes and I leave the canteen. As I walk towards the boxing section, the foreman comes out onto the walkway and hits the railing with his *rotan*.

"Go back to your regular stations!" he shouts. "The thief has been found!"

Then he marches back into his office and slams the door.

There is a lot of noise and confusion as all the workers try to reach their stations. The aisles are too narrow for so many people, and one girl shrieks as she is tripped and trampled on. By the time I finally sit down at my sewing machine, Rochy is already hard at work on a pair of boots.

"It looks like we won't be getting that reward," I say.

Rochy doesn't say anything.

He doesn't even look at me.

What if he spoke to the foreman when I was on my break? What if he told him what he saw me doing?

No, Rochy would never do that.

I start sewing an upper, but every few seconds I look round to see if anyone is missing. I desperately want to know who spoke to the foreman. Maybe the Dragon is sitting in the office right now.

Eventually, the foreman emerges and strides along the walkway. I try not to stare as he walks down the steps and paces across the factory, but I can't help it.

He is still carrying the *rotan*.

The foreman looks straight ahead, tapping the *rotan*

against his leg. As he gets closer I notice he's whistling a tune. When he gets to the end of my row he stops.

Stops walking. Stops whistling. Stops tapping the *rotan*.

Then he turns and heads towards me.

Rochy, how could you?

I look down at my machine. The needle punches stitches into the material. I feel a gust of warm air as the foreman passes me, and as I follow him out of the corner of my eye I notice that Rochy is dripping with sweat.

The foreman suddenly lunges at the girl sitting next to Rochy. She screams as she is dragged from her seat. With one hand clutching her arm, and the other swiping the *rotan* at the back of her thighs, the foreman marches her along the row towards the exit. For the first time I can recall, the factory is completely silent.

Except for the girl's screams and the foreman's angry voice.

And the swish and smack of the *rotan*.

"This will teach you to steal from your employer!" the foreman shouts, his face almost purple with rage. "You'll never work again, do you hear me? You're finished!"

"But it wasn't me," the girl sobs, trying to fend off the *rotan* with her free hand.

"You would say that! All thieves are liars – it's second nature! From what I hear you've been bragging about your crime, promising to do it as many times as you can get away with! I'd whip you all the way to the police station if I thought you were worth the effort! But you're not! You can fend for yourself on the streets, you little *tikus*!"

The girl opens her mouth to say something, but all that comes out is a small wail. Her cheeks shine beneath the electric lights, but her gaping mouth is black.

"What is it?" the foreman says, shaking her arm and holding her on the spot. "Have you got something to say for yourself? Come on then, let's hear it! Everyone is listening!"

The girl gasps, trying to catch her breath. Finally she mumbles, "What about my family?"

The foreman laughs. "What about your family?" He suddenly becomes angry again. "What about them!" He squeezes the girl's arm until she shrieks. "You should have thought about your family before you started stealing from me! I'm sure you can support them with the proceeds of your theft! Now get out of my sight!"

The foreman pushes the girl through the door, giving her one final blow with the *rotan*. He slams the door shut and turns back to face the room.

"What are you all looking at?" he says, wiping the spit from round his mouth. "Get back to work, or you'll be out on the street with that piece of rubbish!"

Suddenly, all the usual factory noises return – the hum of machines, the rustle of paper, the creak of chairs. But above them all is the girl outside, crying and moaning and banging on the door.

The foreman crosses the factory and climbs the stairs to his office. He leans the *rotan* against the wall outside and quietly closes the door.

My heart beats so hard it feels as though my entire body is shaking. When I look across at Rochy's pale face, his hair spiked with sweat, I know better than to say anything. Instead we work in silence, listening to the girl wailing in the street outside.

When I get home, I don't tell anyone about my day.

# IN THE GHETTO

I go outside to practise kick-ups, but my thoughts keep drifting to the girl who stole the boots. I can still hear the sound of the *rotan* slicing through the air. The sound the girl made as it left red stripes on her skin. I know the Dragon must have paid her to steal the boots for his brother – it's too much of a coincidence for the Dragon not to be involved – but something still doesn't seem to add up.

My kick-ups aren't adding up either. The ball bounces on the ground again, throwing up a little puff of dust. I wipe the sweat from my face. I just can't concentrate. Football is a lonely game to play on your own, and I know that with Uston as my sworn enemy, and Fachry and Widodo not much better, I can't afford to fall out with Rochy.

I decide to visit Rochy's apartment. I take my football in case he wants to train and Grandma gives me a bag of pumpkin seeds to share with him. I dribble the ball all the way, dodging people and piles of rubbish. At one point I have to hurdle a bin that has been tipped over. There is a trail of litter across the road, and a few cats and children pick at empty cans and packets. They don't even look up as I race past.

When I reach Rochy's I hide the pumpkin seeds behind my back and knock on the door. After a few seconds I hear someone shuffling on the other side. Then it goes quiet. I'm about to knock again when the door suddenly opens and Rochy's mum looks down at me with a frown. Her hair hangs in greasy strands and her face is wrinkled and yellow like old paper.

"What is it?" she says. "What do you want?"

Her breath smells awful.

"It's me," I say. "Budi. Rochy's friend. I've come to see him."

She looks down at the football beneath my foot and shakes her head.

"You know he's too old to play silly games like football. He's the man of the house now. Haven't you got other friends you could play with instead?"

I shrug. Football is not a silly game. Then I remember the pumpkin seeds and offer the open bag to Rochy's mum.

"Would you like a pumpkin seed, *Ibu*?" I ask.

She peers into the bag and quickly lifts it out of my hand. She starts splitting the seeds between her teeth and spitting the shells onto the ground.

"I'll go and tell him you're here," she says.

I reach out my hand to take the bag back, but she turns away into the gloomy apartment and disappears from sight. She leaves the door open and I can see that the room is a mess. It looks as though someone has emptied a bin onto the middle of the floor. After about a minute she comes back to the doorway, scratching her elbow. The bag of seeds is nowhere to be seen.

"He's not in. He must be at the dump."

Then she closes the door.

I start dribbling in the direction of the dump, but I keep the ball close to me. The dump is surrounded by slums, and the people here live by different rules. Rochy says they ask three questions whenever they find something: "Can I eat it? Can I sell it? Can I burn it?" And the dark shapes huddled in doorways would probably take one look at my football and answer "Yes" to all three.

As I get closer to the dump, the buildings seem to shrink until they are little more than blackened huts, patched together with bits of corrugated metal and plastic sheeting. I pass a naked baby wailing on a piece of cardboard, but no one pays any attention. A murky canal runs from the dump into the slums and I have to pinch my nose against the stench. I notice a group of old men squatting over the water's edge, and further downstream a kid wades after plastic bottles that can be sold by the kilo. I pick up my football just in case it rolls into the water and jog the rest of the way.

The dump is where the city piles all its rubbish, and it smells even worse than the canal. Luckily I spot Rochy by the gate so I don't have to go inside.

"What are you doing here?" he asks.

He looks really surprised to see me.

"Your mum sent me. I went to your apartment to see if you wanted to train and she said I'd find you here." I suddenly notice the black rubbish bag in his hand. "Why have you got that?"

He looks down at the bulging sack in his filthy hand. Something has pierced through the bottom, and every few seconds it drips, leaving a dark splash on the dusty road.

"They wouldn't let me dump it," he says. "The man said I've been coming too often, even though I haven't been here in weeks. I think he's confusing me with someone else."

"Can't you leave it by the gate?" I ask.

Rochy looks round. "I don't think so. I'll have to take it home and try again tomorrow."

We walk back to his apartment. As we pass the canal I pinch my nose again, but Rochy's free hand stays by his side. The streets are darker now, and it's only when we pass a fire on the pavement that I can see Rochy beside me. The rest of the time I can only hear the rustling of the bag as it brushes against his leg.

"Rochy, what's going on? It feels as though everyone is becoming my enemy. Even you seem different. What's happening?"

Someone splashes petrol onto a fire, and in the bright flash I see how tired he looks.

"Is it because Barcelona are ahead of us in the table?" I ask. "If it is then don't worry, because I know we can still win the league. It's a long season."

Rochy makes a noise, but I can't tell whether it's the rustling of the bag or a sigh. "No, Budi," he says. "It's got nothing to do with football."

"Well, what is it then?"

"I'm just bored of it all."

"Bored of what?"

"Of everything. Working in the factory, sharing a room with my mum and sisters. It feels like I'm constantly waiting for something that's never going to happen."

"It could be worse," I say. "What would you do if you didn't have a job at all? What if you lost your job like that girl who was caught stealing? Things would be a lot worse then."

We arrive outside Rochy's apartment and he puts the bag down against the wall.

"Come on," he says. "I don't feel like going inside just yet."

We walk around the corner to a tiny courtyard that is lit by a bulb above a brown door. I pass the ball to Rochy and he starts doing kick-ups. I watch the ball as Rochy loops it from one foot to the other.

"Do you really think that girl stole those boots?" he asks, concentrating on the ball.

"Of course. The foreman said she'd been boasting about it, which is a really stupid thing to do in my opinion. And the Dragon said he would pay someone to do it if I didn't. It makes sense."

"But don't you think it's a bit of a coincidence that lots of people were jealous of her for being so pretty? She wasn't very popular with some of the women."

"What do you mean?"

"I mean that lots of people probably wanted to get rid of her."

"So you don't think she did it?"

Rochy almost loses control of the ball, but manages to keep it off the ground.

"No, I don't," he says. "I know she didn't."

"How do you know?" I ask.

"I just know."

Rochy loops the ball over and I control it on my chest.

"What do you think you'll be doing in ten years' time?" he asks.

"Playing for Real Madrid. Obviously. Maybe I'll be captain."

Rochy laughs. "Do you think you'll be able to get me a season ticket?"

"Of course. I'll get one for you and Mum and Dad and Grandma. We'll all move to Spain."

"That sounds good to me. What number will you be?"

"Eleven. Unless Kieran Wakefield is still in the team, which he probably will be. In that case I'd have to pick something else. Maybe one hundred and eleven."

I lose concentration and the ball bounces in the dust. The light bulb above the door buzzes and flickers.

"How about you?" I ask. "What will you be doing ten years from now?"

Rochy nudges the ball against one of the concrete walls, alternating from right to left foot.

"I don't know." He smiles as though he's about to say something else, but instead he just repeats, "I don't know."

We start doing kick-ups again, but after a few minutes the bulb goes out completely and we're forced to stop.

"I should be getting home," Rochy says. "Mum will want to know where I've been hiding."

We walk back to his apartment, but just before he opens the door he stops and turns to look at me.

"Thanks for coming to see me, Budi. You're right – things could be a lot worse."

He smiles and disappears inside. As I turn to leave, I notice a trail of dark spots leading to Rochy's door. The bag of rubbish has gone.

The streets are empty and quiet. I turn my pockets out to show I'm not worth robbing. Occasionally someone drives past on a scooter, or I hear people arguing in one of the buildings, but otherwise it feels as though I'm alone in the city.

As I get closer to home there is enough light to dribble the rest of the way. I race along the pavement, twisting and turning among imaginary defenders. *He goes past one…and another! He's through on goal! The fans are on their feet! He must score!* I do a 360-degree spin around the corner and run straight into a group of people. The force knocks me over, and I struggle to get back to my feet.

"Hey, watch where you're going, kid."

A jet of red saliva hits the ground beside me. Little pink bubbles squirm and burst on the surface.

"Little Lazaro!" a familiar voice says.

A big, bejewelled hand reaches down and pulls me up by my T-shirt. I look from the Dragon's smirking face to the three brothers behind him. I recognize two of them from the Dragon's house, and the third must be the Chief Inspector, judging by his uniform.

The Dragon releases my shirt and turns to the Chief Inspector.

"This is the kid I was telling you about. The one who works at the factory but is going to be a famous footballer one day."

They all laugh loudly, showing off their little red teeth. One of them has his foot resting on my football.

I gulp. Now they'll make me pay for failing to steal the boots.

"What are you doing out here on your own?" the Chief Inspector asks. "I hope you're not up to no good again."

He smirks as he chews his *sirih*. Then he spits at my feet.

"Hey, Boaz," the Dragon says. "Pass the ball to me."

The men spread around me and pass the ball with big, clumsy kicks.

"Try and get it off us, Little Lazaro!"

The Dragon's Clan are really terrible at football. They make grunting noises whenever the ball comes near them. It doesn't take long for one of them to pass it too close to me and I stick my leg out and pick it up.

"That's handball!" Bayu shouts. "You cheated."

He makes a move towards me but the Dragon holds up a hand.

"Leave it," the Dragon says. "Be nice to Little Lazaro. He's a good boy, after all."

The Dragon holds my chin in his hand and smiles. Then he pats me lightly on the cheek.

"Come on. Let's go."

The brothers walk around me, but Bayu grabs the ball as he passes and kicks it far down the street. His brothers laugh as I run after it.

"Hey, Little Lazaro!" Boaz shouts. "My son loves his boots! He says he's going to be a footballer when he grows up, just like you!"

The men's laughter echoes between the buildings long after they've disappeared from sight. I pick my football out of the gutter and try to make sense of what I just heard. I stand still for a long time before I understand.

And it's only then that I realize how Rochy knew the girl wasn't a thief.

# NEVER BEEN TO SPAIN

There's a rumour going round that a factory collapsed yesterday. Apparently they put a new machine on the top floor and it brought the whole building down. Quite a few people were killed. The last time this happened some white men in suits came and paid off the dead people's families. They became the richest people in town, and it was like they were famous, because all their friends and neighbours kept pestering them for money.

The collapse is really controversial because the factory can't make anything until it has been rebuilt. Apparently the factory where Fachry, Uston and Widodo work is being kept open overnight to try and catch up. Hopefully someone has told the footballers not to get rid of their boots this week, because they might not be getting a new pair for a while. If the message arrives too late they'll probably have to borrow a pair from the substitutes. It would be a disaster if the football got cancelled because there was a shortage of boots. At least Kieran Wakefield would be able to play, because I make his.

I ask Rochy why the footballers who wear the other boots can't use ours until the factory's been rebuilt.

He looks at me and frowns. "They're not allowed!"

"Why not?"

"Because! It's pretty much the worst thing a footballer can do! If a footballer is seen wearing boots with the wrong logo, he'll be in big trouble! It's like Wakefield being seen in a Barcelona shirt!"

Despite the heat of the factory, I shiver at the thought. This logo business seems a bit silly to me. The worst thing a footballer can do is dive, or get a straight red card for punching the referee, or miss a penalty in a Cup Final. Obviously wearing your worst enemy's shirt is pretty bad, but that's got nothing to do with logos.

I must look confused, because Rochy says, "Remember when we talked about the bribes?"

I tell him I remember, even though it still doesn't make much sense to me. Rochy frowns hard at his machine, and I can see he doesn't want to talk any more.

I still haven't spoken to him about stealing the boots for me, partly because I don't know what to say, and partly because the longer I leave it the more I think it's better that he doesn't know I know.

Up on the walkway, outside the foreman's office, the *rotan* leans against the wall. It hasn't been touched since it was used on the girl yesterday.

I wipe the sweat from my forehead and concentrate on the upper I'm stitching. I decide to make as many boots as possible just in case there is a shortage and everyone decides it's okay to wear our boots. Surely they would rather play football in the wrong boots than cancel all the matches. That would be a nightmare. I wouldn't want to be the man in charge of rearranging a hundred football matches.

Then I remember the football boot museum where all the old pairs are kept and realize they will just use those. I feel relieved and stop working quite so fast. My head throbs from the noise of the machines, and I can feel my T-shirt sticking to my back. When the buzzer goes for my break I go outside to get some air.

The sun beats down and there's hardly any shade. It's so hot and humid that I don't feel like eating. Rochy is on the same break so I suggest we play football for a bit.

"We haven't got a ball," he says, wiping his face on his Manchester United shirt.

There's not enough time to run home and fetch mine so I look round for something else.

"We can use this," I say, kicking a plastic bottle towards him.

"It's too hot."

"Come on, Rochy. You can go in goal – all you have to do is stand there."

He shrugs and we go round to the side of the factory. Football is called football because you use your feet, not because you need a football to play. It's obviously better to play with one, but you can use empty bottles, sticks, stones – pretty much anything that moves when you kick it.

There isn't anything better than the bottle round the side so we use that. Rochy stands in front of one of the big bins and I take penalties against him. I like shooting against Rochy because he's quite a bit taller than Fachry, which makes it a lot harder.

In total I take twenty-seven penalties and score fifteen of them. That doesn't seem like a lot but it takes me about five shots to get used to the shape of the bottle, and the bin is only a bit wider than Rochy standing with his arms

out. He only saves four penalties and the rest go wide –
but not by much.

The buzzer goes as the bottle pings off the bin for the
fifteenth time. I make the heart shape with my fingertips
and pat my chest where the Real Madrid badge should
be. Rochy picks the bottle up and turns to put it in the
bin.

"Hey, Budi," he says, "come here."

I walk over and stand on tiptoe to see into the bin.

Inside, scraps of badly cut uppers and snapped sole
units and frayed multicoloured shoelaces form a great
mound of colour. And among them all is a bundle of grey
rags. And among the rags is a man. Nestled within the
crook of his arm is an empty glass bottle, which he cradles
like a baby. A chemical smell of plastic and alcohol rises
from the bin, and I have to turn my face away.

I look at Rochy in disbelief.

"How could anyone sleep through that penalty shoot-
out?" I ask.

Rochy peers into the bin again.

"He's drunk. Excuse me, *Bapak*. Hello!"

The homeless man doesn't stir. Rochy moves to the
side so that the sun falls directly onto his face. Still he
doesn't move.

I edge closer to Rochy. "He's not…dead, is he?"

Rochy leans in and shakes him by the shoulder. The man flinches, grabbing hold of the empty bottle with both hands.

"Away!" he shouts, slurring so much he makes it sound like several words.

"We're going to be late," I say to Rochy. "He's awake now – we know he's okay. Let's go."

"You need to get out of this bin, *Bapak*," Rochy says, ignoring me. He reaches in but the man shrinks away, still cradling the bottle. His bloodshot eyes struggle to focus in the sunlight.

"Monsoooooon," the man says, lifting the empty bottle to his lips.

"It's not the rainy season yet," Rochy says. "We need to get you out, otherwise you'll get crushed when they come to take the rubbish away. That's if you don't cook in here first. Now, come on."

The man finally seems to notice that his bottle is empty, and he abandons it without a second glance. He manages to roll onto all fours and together we haul him out of the bin. As we lower him onto the ground, his long, greasy hair drags across my face.

"He doesn't look well," Rochy says.

I agree. He looks like he might throw up or pass out at any moment.

"At least he's out of that bin," Rochy says. "Now we really need to get back."

"Hang on," I say, acting on a sudden idea. I dig into my pockets and find a few notes. "I'll be back in a minute."

"Where are you going?" Rochy calls after me.

I run around the side of the factory and stop at the first street stall I find. When the vendor sees my money he reaches under his sizzling *wajan* and retrieves a bottle of water from an ice bucket. I hand over the cash and race back to Rochy. The homeless man has thrown up – his legs are covered in a slick, watery sick – and I can tell that Rochy is trying hard not to retch.

"Here," I say, offering the water to the homeless man.

He looks up, and for the first time his eyes focus on me.

"Thank you," he says, taking the bottle and swallowing half the contents in three thirsty gulps.

"Take care," I say, and then Rochy pulls me away. We run back to our stations, hoping our lateness might go unnoticed. But the foreman is like a god – he knows everything.

"Lazy pigs, the both of you!" he shouts, hitting me

across the back of the head. "Who do you think you are, taking an extra five minutes? Do it again and you'll be on break permanently, understand?"

"Yes, *Bapak*."

"Good, now get back to work!"

I reach for the next upper, but I stop short as the sound of the *rotan* slices through the air. Then there's the sickening, breathless shock, like I'm falling from a great height. And then comes the pain, like landing in a pit of needles.

"Rochy!" the foreman shouts. "Make sure you don't wear that shirt tomorrow – we're having an inspection! If the boss sees it he won't be happy, and it'll be me that pays the price!"

And the smack of the *rotan* comes again.

"Yes, *Bapak*," Rochy says, wincing against the pain.

The foreman spends the whole afternoon standing on the walkway, glaring down at us. We're both glad when the day is over.

On the walk home, I ask Rochy why he thinks we're having an inspection.

"Do you reckon they want to make sure our factory won't collapse like the other one?"

Rochy shakes his head. "They've never worried about

it before. The last time we had an inspection they were only interested in how fast the production line was. They fired a bunch of people for being too slow, remember?"

I do remember. A white woman in a man's suit walked around with the foreman, a clipboard in her hand. Whenever she came across something – or someone – she didn't like, she would point her pen at it and make a note on the clipboard. The foreman does a lot of bowing and smiling when we have an inspection, and he makes sure we know to do the same.

I start to wonder why Rochy isn't allowed to wear his Manchester United shirt tomorrow.

"Does the inspector support Manchester City? Or Liverpool? Or Arsenal?"

Manchester United have a lot of worst enemies.

"No," Rochy says. "It's because of the logo. The inspector doesn't like it."

I wonder whether Rochy has taken a bribe.

"But you're not a footballer so it doesn't matter."

Rochy shrugs. He seems really down about it. It is his best shirt, after all.

"Don't worry," I say. "I'm sure you can wear it after tomorrow."

Then I have a really good idea to cheer him up.

"You know the pay rise everyone is talking about?"

"Yeah."

"I wasn't going to say anything, but I'm planning to save as much of the extra money as I can to go and see Kieran Wakefield play at the Bernabéu. If I save enough you could come with me, and I'll buy you a brand-new Real Madrid shirt with *BELMONTE* on the back."

My idea obviously isn't that good, because Rochy looks sadder than ever.

"Budi, you'll never have enough money to do that."

"I will if I save hard enough. With the pay rise we'll get almost 280,000 rupiah a week. Kieran Wakefield only gets 360,000 euros."

Rochy stops walking then. He frowns at me.

"Budi, euros are worth a lot more than rupiah. Just like dollars or pounds."

I frown back. "What do you mean?"

"Come on. Follow me and I'll show you."

We walk to Rochy's apartment in silence. He has a calculator that his dad used when he was a successful salesman, before he died. It's missing a few buttons but it still works.

Rochy rummages inside a cupboard and eventually finds the calculator. He has a good brain for sums so I let him do all the working out. He says that one euro is worth the same as about 16,500 rupiah.

"If Kieran Wakefield earns 360,000 euros a week that would be…"

He shows me the calculator screen. I can't say the number but it looks like this:

**5,940,000,000**

"Five billion, nine hundred and forty million rupiah," Rochy says.

"A week?"

Rochy nods.

That's a lot of rupiah. I always knew footballers were rich, but I didn't know they were *that* rich. The only other time I've heard Rochy talk about billions was when he tried to explain how many stars are in the sky. A billion is a lot.

Rochy goes quiet and pushes a lot of buttons and scratches his head.

"I'm not sure," he says, "but I think it takes Kieran Wakefield a hundred seconds to earn as many rupiah as we earn in a month."

We decide that the calculator probably is broken after all.

# 11 THINGS YOU COULD DO IN 100 SECONDS

1. Get out of bed and get dressed.
2. Eat breakfast.
3. Run from home to the factory.
4. Sew the upper of one boot.
5. Lace two pairs of boots.
6. Go for a toilet break at the factory.
7. Put the insoles in ten pairs of boots.
8. Box fifteen pairs of boots.
9. Run home from the factory.
10. Eat dinner.
11. Get undressed and ready for bed.

# IF I CAN DREAM

The foreman is wearing his suit. The jacket is too big and it hangs off his shoulders, making him look like a child pretending to be a grown-up. Every few minutes he wipes the sweat from his face with a stained handkerchief. He paces along the rows, his eyes constantly searching for someone to pounce on, barking at anyone who so much as glances up from their work.

Usually, inspectors are late. Or they don't show up at all. Once the foreman wore his suit for two weeks before giving up hope of a visit.

But today, for some reason, the inspector is early. There is a loud banging on the corrugated door, and the foreman glares at us one final time before opening it.

Usually, the foreman rushes out to meet the inspector

as though they are his favourite person. He shakes their hand and bows and ushers them into the factory.

But today, for some reason, he stands speechless in the doorway. It is only when he moves aside, stumbling over his own shoes, that we see why.

Instead of a single person, a group of men – ten of them – enter the factory and line up along the wall. I can tell they aren't inspectors because they are Indonesian rather than white, and they are wearing army uniforms instead of suits.

After the last soldier has entered, a man with a moustache and a beret closes the door and shouts an order at them. He must be the commanding officer. Eight of the soldiers turn at the same time and march round the edge of the factory, their rifles balanced against their shoulders. Two of them wait by the door, holding their guns across their chests. So many workers have stopped to watch that I can hear the stomp of the soldiers' boots on the concrete floor.

They march all the way round the room and up the stairway that leads to the foreman's office. The officer strolls behind them and beckons for the foreman to follow him. When they come to a stop on the walkway and stamp their feet, the foreman scurries alongside and unlocks the door. After surveying the factory, the officer takes three soldiers into the room, leaving the other five on the walkway. Everyone looks up at the stern soldiers, wondering what will happen next.

Slowly, we all return to our work.

After several minutes of waiting, the office door opens and one of the soldiers strides onto the balcony with a piece of paper. Everyone stops working and the soldier calls out a name. The factory falls completely silent.

No humming machines.

No rustling paper.

No barked orders.

Then a chair scrapes, and someone at the far end of the factory walks across the floor and up the stairs towards the soldiers. She looks terrified. Just before she reaches the office, the foreman comes out and shouts, "Keep working!"

Everyone busies themselves with their tasks, but I can tell no one is really concentrating.

The foreman follows the petrified woman into the office, closing the door behind him. Gradually, the sewing machine needles come to a stop as we all watch the walkway. The soldiers fiddle with their rifles and make jokes that I can't hear. One of them takes aim and pretends to spray bullets over the balcony. The other soldiers laugh.

After less than a minute the office door opens and the woman walks quickly back to her station. There is a surge of noise from the sewing machines as everyone pretends to work again. The soldiers straighten up and look serious as their comrade calls another name. This time a tiny old woman, who looks like she's spent her entire life hunched over a sewing machine, stands and shuffles to the office.

The door has only just closed behind her when the sounds of an argument inside the room silence the sewing machines. The voices get louder, all speaking at once. Then there is a shriek and a thud. A moment later the office door opens and two soldiers emerge, supporting the old woman between them. Her mouth is covered in blood and her head lolls from side to side. As the soldiers carry her downstairs her shins drag against the steps. She groans faintly.

One of the workers by the cutting machine, a big man named Haliim, steps forward to intervene. The soldiers on the walkway raise their rifles and threaten to shoot him.

"Then why don't you kill me, you cowards!" he shouts, holding out his arms.

A murmur spreads through the factory. Someone else demands to know what's going on, and it's not until the officer appears on the balcony, holding his pistol in the air, that order is restored. Someone drags Haliim back before he can cause any more trouble.

When the soldiers with the old lady reach the exit, they open the door and dump her onto the street outside. They close the door and return to the office upstairs. We are told to carry on working.

Then the same thing happens all over again. A name is called. Someone shuffles up the staircase. A minute later the person reappears. Another name is called.

And every time it feels as though someone is about to twist the knife inside.

Only one other person ends up being dumped on the street: Haliim. It takes four soldiers to subdue him, and he thrashes around as they half-carry, half-drag him across the factory. And all the while one of them jabs at him with the butt of a rifle.

The process must happen about twenty times before they call another name that I recognize.

My name.

I look at Rochy and he looks at me like it's his name that's been called.

"Hurry up!" the soldier shouts.

I walk to the staircase and stumble up the steps. I can feel everyone watching me. I feel sick. This is what the walk from the halfway line must be like in a penalty shoot-out. As I pass the line of soldiers one of them pulls a face at me. I look down at my feet. I turn into the office and hear the door close behind me.

This is the first time I've been inside the foreman's office. Now I can see why he's always prowling around the factory floor – I wouldn't want to spend much time in here either. There's a dead plant in one corner, an overflowing bin in the other, and a desk in the centre of the room. The foreman sits behind the desk with a strange expression on his face. Three soldiers stand against the back wall and the officer waits beside the desk, a fat cigar sticking out from beneath his moustache.

The foreman points a hand at the seat opposite him. There are a few spots of blood beneath it.

"Please take a seat, Budi."

He's never been polite to me before. I sit down.

"All we need you to do is put your name on this form."

The foreman's eye twitches as a bead of sweat rolls down one side of his nose. His face glistens under the electric strip light. Grandma would say he's sweating like

Elvis, because apparently Elvis used to get really hot when he was singing onstage. She showed me a magazine clipping once. I never knew someone so sweaty could be so popular. I look down at the form on the desk.

"What does it say?"

The foreman's expression changes. His lips uncurl slightly, and his eyebrows bunch together.

"Budi, just sign the form and you can go back to work."

I hesitate because I don't have a signature. I've never had to sign anything before. On the foreman's desk there is a picture of a woman and two children that catches my attention. It looks like they're at the zoo. There's something in a cage behind them, but as I lean closer a hand slams down onto the desk, knocking it over. The hand doesn't move, and I look along the uniformed sleeve to the round moustached face leaning over me. The officer takes the cigar out of his mouth and blows a cloud of smoke into my face.

"Trust me," he says quietly, "you want to sign that form."

I cough once. The foreman turns to the officer and puts his hand up.

"He'll sign the form. It's okay." Then he turns to me. "Sign the form, Budi. All it says is that you don't want the pay rise."

"But I do want the pay rise. I'm going to use the money to visit Spain and watch Real Madrid play at the Bernabéu."

The officer holds his cigar between two fingers and turns to the soldiers at the back of the room. He smiles, and they all start laughing. They laugh quietly at first, a bit at a time, but then they can't control themselves. The foreman laughs too, but I can tell he doesn't think it's that funny. I don't get the joke either. When they eventually stop, the officer wipes his eyes with a knuckle.

"You're funny, kid," he says. "That's the best."

The foreman leans across the desk and picks up the pen.

"Budi. Just sign the form. Please."

And that's when I realize the foreman doesn't want me to sign the form; he *needs* me to sign the form. I see for the first time how above the foreman is another foreman, with a *rotan* that swishes and stings just as much as his own. I look at the fallen photo frame on the desk and begin to see how he is just doing what he has to do. Surviving, like everyone else. The foreman obeys the soldiers, the soldiers obey the officer, the officer obeys the General. And beneath them all, obeying them all, is me.

"Please," the foreman says. "Just do it."

I'm about to tell him that I don't have a signature when I finally get the joke: the calculator was right. And then I feel it – the first trickle of blood seeping out of a new cut, somewhere deep in my chest. And I already know it will bleed for ever. That it will drip just enough to never stop, but never enough to kill me.

I take the pen and imagine that all these soldiers are here to protect me from crazy fans, and that the form is a contract to play for Real Madrid for 360,000 euros a week.

Slowly, carefully, I copy Kieran Wakefield's autograph onto the paper.

The soldiers start laughing again as I leave the office, but I just ignore them. People with guns can get away with laughing at pretty much anybody.

When I get back to my station, Rochy asks me about what happened and I tell him that we aren't getting the pay rise. He nods and carries on with his stitching.

I ask him whether he thinks I could make it as a professional footballer.

"Maybe," he says. "It's hard to tell."

\* \* \*

When I get home, Mum and Dad are arguing. Dad sits with his back to me, gesturing at something on the table I can't see. Mum stands with her hands on her hips, shaking her head. It looks as though she's been crying. Grandma is slumped in her armchair, staring at the threadbare rug. She doesn't seem to notice me even though I'm right in front of her.

"I don't know, Elvis!" Mum shouts. "I don't know what any of this means for us!"

"It's bad news, that's for sure. They'll come here, you know that?"

"Don't say that!" Mum says, turning away.

"But it's true!"

"Isn't there something we can do? What if we went to the Dragon?"

"No," Grandma says, so quietly that it's somehow more shocking than all the shouting. She is still staring at the floor, as though hypnotized by the pattern on the rug. "We don't go anywhere. If they must come here, let them come."

Mum and Dad turn to look at her, and their eyes widen when they see me waiting by the door. Dad rushes to conceal whatever is on the table and Mum wipes her eyes and forces a smile.

"Budi," she says. "How long have you been standing there?"

"What's going on?" I ask, ignoring her question.

"Nothing," Dad says, looking over his shoulder. "Why don't you go outside and play for a while? We're just having a grown-up conversation."

I hate it when I'm left out for being a kid. If only they knew about the grown-up conversation I've already had today. I clench my fists against the swelling anger in my chest, and resist the urge to tell them what happened at the factory.

"It's not *playing*," I say through gritted teeth. "It's *training*."

"We don't have time for this!" Dad shouts, slamming his hand onto the table and turning to face me. As he stands I get a glimpse of what he was blocking from my view. It's a folded newspaper, although I can't see why he wanted to hide it.

"I just want to know what's going on!" I shout back.

"Don't talk back to me like that!" he says. "This is a family matter! It's none of your business! Now do as I say!"

My mouth falls open.

How can a family matter be none of my business?

I can tell Dad already regrets saying it, but rather than listen to his apology I storm out of the apartment and run through the maze of side streets, turning this way and that so no one will be able to find me. My head feels thick with rage and tears and I have no idea where I'm going. All I know is that I want to get away. The anger keeps my legs moving, but no matter how far I run I can still hear Dad's words just as clearly as when they were first spoken.

I reach a part of the city where the crowded backstreets become wider, and the buildings on either side grow taller. The windows have glass in them. The walls are newly painted. An electric light illuminates every room. And, up ahead, the skyscrapers of the rich district glow against the darkening sky. I must have run a long way.

At the end of the street the buildings give way to a large, floodlit rectangle.

And then I realize where my feet are taking me.

The football academy.

As I get closer I hear echoed shouting. Someone claps encouragement, and the crisp thud of a football being thumped is met with cheers. I hook my fingers onto the wire fence surrounding the pitch and rest my head against the mesh.

Beneath the floodlights, the pitch looks thick and

luscious and flat and slick. I wonder how it stays so wet when it hasn't rained in months. The ball, shiny from the moisture of the pitch, glides from one pair of boots to another. The boots shine too, and I recognize the fluorescent yellows and lime greens and bright oranges from the factory.

I wonder what it would be like to play football on grass.

The players must be about Rochy's age – fourteen or fifteen – but they are as big as men and just as strong. One of the wingers makes a run on the far side of the pitch and a midfielder chases him down. I hear the winger hit the ground from where I'm standing and half expect him to roll around, clutching his ankle. But within a second he's up and chasing after the ball.

On the touchline, a man with a whistle around his neck scribbles on a notepad. He must have taken a bribe because everything – from his boots to his tracksuit to his baseball cap – is covered in the same logo.

On the pitch, a player who is much smaller than everyone else races towards a line of defenders. He keeps the football close to his feet and twists and turns past tackle after tackle. As he surges into the box, the goalkeeper rushes to close him down. One of the attacker's teammates urges him to square the ball for an open goal. But the small player shoots instead, and the keeper punches the shot away.

"Hey, kid," a voice says. "What are you doing?"

I look along the fence and watch as an old man makes his way towards me. His overalls are dirty, and he carries a sack in one hand and a tube in the other. Every few paces he shakes the tube and sprinkles something on the ground. To my surprise he has a pair of brand-new football boots on his feet – real ones – but he looks far too old to play.

"I asked you a question," he says, stopping a few paces from me.

"I'm just watching the match," I say.

The man frowns at me, but soon turns to look at the pitch. The small player is on the ball again, trying to dribble out of his own penalty area.

"He'll be a star one day," the man says, nodding in the direction of the boy as he skips over an outstretched leg. "One of the greats. Victor, he's called. Remember the name."

I shake my head. "He'll never be great if he doesn't learn to pass the ball."

The man raises his eyebrows. "So you're an expert on the beautiful game, are you?"

I shrug. "You don't have to be an expert. Football is a team game. It helps if you're a team player."

Victor is muscled off the ball by two big defenders and tumbles to the floor. He rolls over, holding his shoulder, but when he realizes no one is paying attention he gets up and wanders back to the halfway line.

"Anyway, what are *you* doing here?" I ask. "And where did you get those boots?"

The man laughs. "I'm the groundskeeper," he says. "And I got these boots from my employer. I need to wear them to protect the pitch. That's why I've got these as well." He holds up the sack and the tube. "Lots of vermin like the look of my beautiful grass. Rats want to burrow and make their nests. Cats want to dig holes and *berak* everywhere. That's why I'm putting poison around the perimeter."

"And the sack?"

He taps the bulge at the bottom of the sack.

"I'll let you work that one out for yourself."

Over on the pitch, Victor is rolling around again. This time it's his shin.

"How do you get the grass to look like that?" I ask.

"Water," he says. "Lots of water. And plenty of patience. Looks good, doesn't it?"

I nod. "I bet it's even better to play on."

The groundskeeper smiles. "You reckon you're good enough to take on these guys?"

"I don't know." I squeeze the wire fence beneath my fingers. "But it doesn't matter. I'd never be able to afford it."

"It doesn't cost anything if you're good enough. Some of these kids come from the slums. They get sponsored to train here."

"But my family needs me to work. My grandmother needs a lot of medicine."

The groundskeeper yawns. "Listen, kid. I've worked here a long time. I've seen hundreds of boys come through the academy. Some of them went on to be professionals. Some of them didn't. But the ones that made it had one thing in common."

He pauses, and I can tell he wants me to make a guess.

"They were really talented?"

"No. They had the right attitude. What you said about Victor might be true," he says, looking over at the boy who is still rolling around. "He's good enough to make it, but if he doesn't acquire the right attitude he's got no chance."

"But my family..." I say. "If I just had enough money to train here until someone sponsored me—"

"Kid, I've heard it all before. Sure, your family needs you to earn. But there will always be something in the way. You know, I've been putting poison down for years. And do you know how many rat nests I've found beneath the pitch? Or how many cat droppings I've picked up from the grass? Zero. They all fall at the first obstacle. And they all end up in this sack. I used to wonder why the rats don't start their burrows outside the perimeter, or why cats don't leap over the ring of poison. It's because they can see what they want, but they can't see past what's stopping them.

"There will always be something – or someone – stopping you from realizing your potential. Always a groundskeeper tending the fence. Always a goalkeeper guarding the goal. You've just got to see beyond him."

The groundskeeper sighs and swings the sack over his shoulder. He sprinkles some pellets on the grass between us.

"The problem with being a dreamer is that occasionally you'll have nightmares – you've just got to make sure they don't ever spook you enough to want to wake up.

"Now, get out of here," he says, smiling. "Before you end up in the sack."

I start walking home, and soon the roads begin to

narrow and crumbling buildings crowd around on either side. Dim street fires replace the bright lights of the academy, and even though the air is bitter with the smell of burning rubbish it feels good to draw deep breaths into my lungs.

A few streets from my apartment I notice a boy curled up in a doorway, sucking his thumb. I'm about to walk past when something catches my eye and makes me stop. The boy is sleeping on a mat of newspaper pages, and just below his outstretched hand there is a picture of a person that I recognize.

It's Dad.

But not as I've ever seen him before. He looks mean, and his eyes stare out from the front page like two black, empty holes.

A faint breeze rustles the sheets and brings the face to life, making me shiver. The boy stirs among the flapping pages and I break into a run. I don't look back.

My heart jumps into my throat when I round the corner and almost crash into Dad.

"Budi, there you are!" He draws me into a strong hug. "I'm sorry, son. I lost my temper and said some things I didn't mean." He releases me and looks into my face. "Where have you been, Budi? You look pale. Are you okay?"

In the darkness, his eyes have that black, empty look about them.

I manage to nod. "I'm fine. Just tired."

"Come on, let's get you home."

Mum and Grandma are both relieved to see me, and I let them hug me before taking myself off to bed.

I collapse onto my mattress and try to make sense of everything. Why would Dad be in the newspaper? They only put your picture in the paper if you've done something really good.

Or something really bad.

And if he's done something good, why would they use a picture that makes him look so bad? Then I remember all the overtime he's done recently, and I wonder whether he really has been working late, or whether he was doing something else instead. Something illegal. I know lots of people do bad things to earn extra money, but I never thought Dad might be one of them.

I close my eyes. I fall asleep. I dream.

And I wake up to the nightmare.

# WHEN IT RAINS, IT REALLY POURS

It's dark. There are people in my room. Men. They're shouting. They reach down and drag me from my bed into a room of more shouting and screaming. Torches flash over the walls. A dog's jaws, wet with stringy saliva, snap at the end of a leash. Black shadows snake across the room. My hands are pulled behind my back. A heavy boot buckles my knees, and I sink to the floor.

I try to beg – "Don't shoot me!" – but nothing comes out, or it gets lost beneath the barking of men and dogs. Outside, a car starts up and races away.

This is how they get you. They come in the middle of the night and drag you out of bed and give you a choice: kneeling or standing?

"Standing," I say. "I want to stand."

"Shut that *kurang ajar* boy up," a voice growls, and a gloved hand smacks me across the face.

I don't say anything after that. I just let my head slump forward and try to block out the sound of crying. I know it's Mum, even in the darkness, because Grandma never cries.

"You can shut her up as well!" the voice says, and for a moment I feel as though I've heard the voice somewhere before.

Then I hear the sound of a gloved hand striking my mother's face.

I try to get up, but a strong arm pulls me back.

"Are they all restrained?"

"Yes, sir."

"Where are the lights?"

"Generator must have died, sir."

"Well, get the emergency lighting out of the van, then! You can't rely on anything in this district. And get that dog to shut up or we'll have the whole neighbourhood here in a minute."

The dog is muzzled, and for a moment the only sound is a quiet sobbing. Then something is dragged through the doorway and a blinding light fills the room. I try to raise my hand to my eyes, but something digs into my wrists and stops me.

Slowly, my eyes adjust to the brightness. Half a dozen men stand around the room, but my eyes are drawn to the one in the centre. The Chief Inspector stands with his hands on his hips, his uniform stretched across his stomach, looking from me to Mum to Grandma. Mum is on her knees on the opposite side of the room, next to the table. Grandma sits in her armchair, her hands cable-tied in her lap, and she stares coolly at the Chief Inspector.

"Where's Dad?" I ask, and the policeman next to me raises his hand in anticipation of the order. But the Chief Inspector waves it away.

"Your father has been taken into custody for questioning."

"But why?" I ask.

This time the Chief Inspector nods. The policeman strikes me with the back of his hand, and my cheek stings from the blow.

"It's okay, Budi," Mum says. "Everything will be all right."

The Chief Inspector smirks. "We'll see about that."

Someone appears in the darkness just beyond the door, and the rest of the policemen stand to attention. The Chief Inspector takes a seat, propping his feet on the table and making it squeak.

"Come in, brother," he says, still smirking. "Don't be shy."

The Dragon steps through the doorway, his gold chains and bejewelled hands glinting in the harsh light. As he passes the police dog he stops to pat it on the head.

"You can untie them," he says, not looking up, and immediately the policemen busy themselves with the cable ties around our wrists. I get up and rush over to hug Mum and Grandma, anger and relief flooding through me.

"Two of you wait in the van," the Chief Inspector says to the policemen. "The rest of you can go."

The policemen file out, and the Dragon sits on the opposite side of the table to his brother. Nobody speaks while the Dragon takes a packet of *sirih* from his pocket and starts chewing. The Chief Inspector picks at something under his nails. My stomach squirms at the thought of them mentioning the stolen football boots in front of my family.

Finally, Grandma breaks the silence.

"What are you doing?" she asks. "What do you mean by coming here and taking my son away?"

The two brothers look at each other, and the Dragon makes a gesture with his hand for the Chief Inspector to answer.

"As I'm sure you're aware," he says, still fiddling with a fingernail, "you have two sons."

I expect Grandma's expression to change, the way it does whenever I accidentally mention my uncle, but she continues to stare at the brothers.

"And I'm sure you're equally aware," the Chief Inspector continues, "that one of your sons recently escaped from his cell on Nusa Kambangan."

Suddenly the picture in the paper makes sense, and the knife inside twists at the thought I ever suspected Dad of doing something bad.

Grandma narrows her eyes at the Chief Inspector.

"And as I'm sure *you're* aware," she says, "Elvis is completely innocent. So why is he under arrest?"

"You see, when a *convict* escapes," the Chief Inspector says, and I notice Grandma flinch slightly, "it is quite common for him to contact his family. More often than not fugitives are caught hiding under their parents' bed, or in the latrine at the back of the family home. It's probably a result of being locked up for so long that they don't know what to do when they get out. They use up all their imagination in the escape attempt. Then they resort to life before their imprisonment."

"I haven't heard from Aaron at all," Grandma says, and

for a moment I get confused. Then I realize that my uncle must be called Aaron. I can't believe I didn't work it out sooner: Elvis Aaron Presley.

"That's what we're investigating," the Chief Inspector says with a smile. "And I'm sure we can rely on your co-operation."

"What do you want us to do?" asks Mum.

"Here's how it's going to work," the Dragon says, sitting forward and spitting a stream of red saliva onto the floor. "At some point Aaron is going to contact you. He doesn't have a choice. He has no one else. And unless you want Elvis to take his place on Nusa Kambangan, I suggest you let us know as soon as Aaron gets in touch."

Grandma laughs, but it's short and bitter.

"You can't expect a mother to sacrifice one son to save another."

"You don't have a choice," the Dragon says. "With Elvis in jail it won't be long before you can't make your rent payments, and then you'll be fending for yourselves in the slums."

Grandma looks down at her hands, folding one over the other.

"And why is it so important that I turn my son over to you?"

"Well," the Chief Inspector says, "recapturing a dangerous criminal—"

"He's not dangerous," Grandma says, her voice rising. "He might be a criminal but he's not dangerous."

"I'll bear that in mind," the Chief Inspector says, smirking. "As I was saying, recapturing a...notorious criminal would go a long way towards furthering my career. With a scalp like that on my record, it wouldn't be long before I was looking at an office in the rich district."

"So *you* can extort politicians and bankers?" Mum asks, glaring at the Dragon.

The Dragon shrugs like he doesn't know what Mum means, but the gold chains around his neck wink at us in the light.

"However," the Dragon says, "if Aaron were to co-operate in a little export project I've been working on, we could help keep him out of prison for good, couldn't we, brother?"

The Chief Inspector scowls but eventually nods his agreement. "That could be arranged."

"So you see," the Dragon continues, creating another red splat on the floor, "it's in everybody's best interests for you to let us know as soon as he gets in touch."

No one replies. The Dragon and the Chief Inspector exchange a glance and stand up.

"You know where to find me," the Dragon says, pausing on his way out to pat my cheek.

The Chief Inspector calls two of the policeman in to remove the light, and after it's been loaded up and driven away we are finally left alone. Dawn is breaking outside, and a ghostly half-light creeps into the room. Mum rushes to the table and starts scrubbing at the *sirih*-spit stains on the floor. I sit down on the rug by Grandma's feet and start playing with the tassels. I wrap them around my finger so tightly the three little needle cuts across my fingertip split open and fresh blood seeps into the tassels. I don't feel any pain.

"What are we going to do?" Mum asks, still scrubbing at the floor.

Grandma shakes her head. "I don't know. I can't choose between my sons."

Mum stops scrubbing and blows a loose hair out of her face.

"They can't be trusted, can they?" she says. "When they say they could keep Aaron out of prison?"

"I don't know," Grandma says. "But I'd have to betray him to find out."

Looking up at Grandma, I notice there are tears in her eyes. Then she says the last thing I expect her to say.

"Would you like to hear a story, Budi?"

"Okay."

Mum stops scrubbing at the floor, even though she hasn't finished removing the stains, and sits back on her heels to listen.

"Once upon a time there was a soldier. He was everything a captain could want from a private – strong, loyal and dependable. The captain trusted the soldier completely, and one day she entrusted something very precious to him. As expected, the soldier took his duty very seriously, and the treasure remained safe in his guardianship.

"But one night, while everyone in the barracks slept, a surprise attack woke the soldier from his slumber. Sluggish with sleep and gripped by panic, he rushed from his bunk to safety, forgetting the treasure in his haste. It was only when he emerged from the building and saw his captain that the soldier realized his mistake. He returned to the barracks but it was already overrun by enemy troops. He could see no way back in. Falling to his knees, he began to weep for the lost treasure when suddenly the major – someone very dear to the captain – emerged with the prize. The soldier and the captain were overjoyed to be reunited with the treasure. But the major was

**193**

gravely injured, and he died shortly afterwards."

A single tear spills over Grandma's cheek, but she doesn't seem to notice.

"This devastated the captain, and in her anger she said many unfair things. She blamed the soldier for the major's death. She called him a coward. She even wished him dead. Grief made the captain blind to all the acts of loyalty and steadfastness for which the soldier was renowned. The captain drove the soldier away, and the soldier ran."

Tears drip from Grandma's chin onto the blanket across her lap. But still she doesn't wipe them away.

"When the captain's fury had subsided, she longed to undo the thoughtless things she had said in grief. She searched for the soldier, but the soldier did not want to be found. He had fled into the wilderness, pushing further and further into the darkness, trying to outrun the hurt he believed he deserved. He fell in with rogues; he broke laws to survive. The captain lost all hope of seeing him again.

"And now this," Grandma mumbles.

My cheeks are wet with tears. Over by the table, Mum cries silently.

A memory from long ago swims up in my mind. I'm

sitting on Grandma's knee, and she's telling me about the time I slept through an earthquake – a huge earthquake – and we laugh at the ridiculousness of the idea. I laugh and laugh at the image of buildings crashing to the ground while I dream peacefully. Grandma laughs with me, but the smile in her eyes dies long before the smile on her lips.

And then I recall another memory. Grandma speaks very seriously about the time Grandpa died in an earthquake. She says if it wasn't for the family curse he probably would have survived, but the hospitals were full and he lost too much blood.

And it never really occurred to me that these stories happened at the same time, that they were both the same story. I knew, but at the same time I didn't know. Didn't understand. In the past I felt annoyed at Grandpa for dying. I felt like he abandoned me. But he carried me to safety when no one else could reach me, when everything was falling apart. And he died doing it.

He saved me.

I have to say it out loud.

"Grandpa saved me."

Grandma blinks and fresh tears roll across her cheeks. But they are for an old hurt. And I know, even though she doesn't have the family curse, I just know she's bleeding on the inside.

And then, outside, I hear the first fat drops of the rainy season. They seem to fall one by one at first, uncertain whether it's the right time. But then they build into a downpour, and the windowsill explodes with raindrops.

We all look out the window as though we've never seen rain before. A cool gust of air – the first in months – drifts through the window, and Grandma takes a deep breath. It rouses Mum as well, who returns to scrubbing the stains from the floor.

"You'd better get ready for work," she says. "You don't want to be late."

Despite Mum's warning I arrive late and soaked through. I expect the foreman to be waiting by my station with his *rotan*, but for some reason he keeps his distance. Maybe he's heard about my uncle who's just escaped from Execution Island. As I walk between the rows I notice that everyone is whispering and glancing over at me. News must travel fast. Maybe Rochy was right. Maybe I wouldn't want to be famous after all.

As I start sewing I can tell that Rochy is watching me. But it's not until there is a pile of finished uppers next to my machine that he leans across and whispers to me.

"I heard about your…your family," he says. "I'm sorry about your dad."

I swallow hard. "Thanks."

Rochy coughs.

"How about you come round for El Clásico tomorrow night? Watching Barcelona get thrashed by Real Madrid should help take your mind off things."

"Okay."

"And we could see if the others want to play a match tonight as well."

"Okay."

I agree because it's easier than resisting. Easier than explaining. But all I can think about is Dad being interrogated in a damp, dark cell. And all I want is for things to be back to normal.

It rains all day. It rains so hard that the drumming of raindrops on the tin roof drowns out the clatter of the sewing machines. I walk home with Rochy through the downpour, and he goes to call for Fachry and Uston and Widodo while I collect my football.

We meet in the square, and I realize I haven't seen any of them since they abandoned me to the Dragon almost a week ago. I know Rochy must have talked to them because they all apologize when they see me. Uston even waits until the game has started to remind me that Real Madrid are below Barcelona in La Liga.

The conditions are really difficult because the ground is slippery and there are puddles everywhere. A small stream of brown water runs in front of the fence we use as a goal, and Fachry has to stand off his line so his shoes don't fill with water. By the time we get started it's raining so hard we have to stop every few minutes to wring out our T-shirts. Eventually we decide to take them off and just play in our shorts.

The game does not go very well for Rochy and me. The puddles make it really difficult to pass to each other because they slow the ball down. One puddle is so deep that it stops the ball completely, and every time it floats on the surface two players splash in to try and win it. It doesn't help that Uston and Widodo are cheats. At one point I'm about to score but Uston kicks my standing foot from under me. I land heavily in a puddle and get some of the gritty water in my eye.

"That's a penalty!" I shout, rubbing my eye with my wrist.

"Shut up!" Uston says. "You dived! Just like Wakefield!"

Fachry is supposed to referee as well as being goalkeeper, but when I ask him whether it's a penalty he shrugs and says that he didn't see it properly.

My eye is burning, and whenever I rub it the pain gets worse.

"Are you crying?" Widodo asks.

"No!" I say, even though I can feel hot tears welling up and mixing with the rainwater on my cheeks. "I've just got something in my eye!"

"Ha!" Uston says. "Don't get upset, Budi, Real Madrid haven't lost the title to Barcelona just yet!"

"Shut up!" Rochy says. "You won't be so smug when you get knocked out of the Copa del Rey!"

Uston pushes Rochy, and for a moment it looks as though a fight is about to break out. Fachry makes a move to separate them, and while he's off his line Widodo blasts the ball against the fence.

"One–nil!" he shouts, looking up and pointing to the dark clouds overhead. Uston turns away from Rochy and puts an arm around Widodo's neck in celebration.

"That doesn't count!" I say. "Fachry, you have to tell them that doesn't count! We weren't even playing!"

Fachry shrugs again and goes to collect the ball.

"What's the matter?" Uston asks. "Afraid you can't come back from a goal down?"

"Whatever," Rochy says. "Come on, let's play!"

My eye is still itchy and sore but we manage to get a goal back almost immediately. Rochy makes a run between Uston and Widodo and I chip it over their heads. Fachry comes out to catch it but Rochy beats him to it and heads the ball into the goal. We don't even bother celebrating.

The rain falls so hard it stings our faces when we follow Fachry's high kick into the air for the restart.

"We'll have to stop soon!" Rochy shouts.

"You can forfeit if you want," Uston says, "but Barca never quit!"

We play on. I can tell everyone is in a bad mood because there are more fouls than passes. At one point Rochy slips in the mud and Widodo kicks him in the side, trying to get the ball from beneath him.

"This is stupid!" I shout. I can hardly see the opposite side of the square through the downpour. "Can't we play the rest of the match when it's not raining so hard?"

"Just because you're scared of losing!" Uston says. "Fine! Next goal wins!"

Fachry kicks the ball out and Rochy manages to head it down to me. Uston lunges at my feet, sliding through a shallow puddle, but I sidestep his tackle and run towards the goal. Widodo chases me but I know he isn't going to catch me in time. Fachry steps forward to block my shot but I pass the ball beyond his outstretched leg.

As I run off to celebrate, my hands in the shape of a heart, I look back at the goal. My heart sinks as I watch the ball stop dead in the stream that runs in front of the fence. It's like watching a horrible slow-motion replay as Widodo hurdles over Fachry and slams the ball into the goal. Uston picks himself up off the floor and runs over to Widodo. He jumps on his back and cheers, shaking his fist in my direction.

"You're both cheats!" I shout.

"I can't hear you!" Uston says, holding his hand to his ear as Widodo carries him around.

"I'm going home," Rochy says, picking up his Manchester United shirt and wringing it out.

"No, we've got to stay and beat them," I say.

"Yeah," says Uston, jumping down from Widodo's back and strutting up to us. "Surely you don't have to go home yet. It's still early. Your sisters won't even be at work."

Rochy's hands curl into fists.

"Don't talk about my family," he says through gritted teeth, his face set against the driving rain.

Uston looks at me and smiles. "Come on, Rochy, we all know what they really do. It's nothing to be ashamed of. Everyone's got to make a living, even if it is as a—"

"One more word and you'll regret it!" Rochy shouts.

He looks like he's about to erupt. Widodo puts a hand on Uston's shoulder as if to pull him away, but Uston doesn't move. He just smirks at me again. When he speaks he savours each word like it's coated in sugar.

"Even if it is as a couple of—"

Rochy's punch beats the word to his lips. And it isn't the kind of punch you sometimes see in a match between Real Madrid and Barcelona. Uston doesn't grab his face and flop around on the floor like a fish out of water. Rochy punches him like a boxer, and Uston falls like a tree. We don't all clamour around Rochy, shoving and swearing and slapping at the air. There is no referee blowing his whistle and waving a red card above his head. We stand like statues, staring at the motionless body between us.

Rochy pulls his Manchester United shirt over his head, fighting to get his arms through the soaked sleeves, and storms off. As he walks away I notice all the letters are peeling away from his back, and the top of the seven hangs off, flapping with every step he takes.

And it's only after he turns the corner that I finally

consider what Uston was about to say. Maybe Rochy's sisters aren't just *pemulung*. Maybe they do something else at night. Maybe they're…

"Rochy!" I shout, setting off after him. "Wait!"

"What about Uston?" Fachry asks, looking at me with wide eyes. Widodo is still staring at his brother.

"Get him home!"

I turn and run, clutching my football to my shirtless body. The rain falls so hard it stings my shoulders, but I run through alley after alley until I catch up with Rochy. Even when I pull alongside him it seems as though he's trying to get away from me.

"Stop walking so fast," I say. "I can't keep up."

He glances at me and walks even faster.

"You should have let me go home when I wanted to. None of that would have happened."

He turns down a narrow alleyway so that I have to walk behind him.

"I'm sorry," I say. "But it doesn't matter what your sisters do—"

Rochy suddenly spins round and points a finger in my face. His eyes are wild.

"You mention my sisters again and I'll knock you out as well, got it?"

He turns away before I can reply, so I shout at the peeling letters on his back instead.

"But we're friends, Rochy! I don't care about what Uston said!"

He keeps walking, but I don't want him to leave like this. So I shout something else.

"Rochy's sisters are liars and I don't care who knows it!"

That gets his attention. He stops. Turns. Strides back towards me. For a moment I think he's going to walk straight over me, but he stops just in time. About an arm's length away.

"Are you going to make me hurt you, Budi?"

Rainwater drips from his nose into the puddle between us. His fists are clenched.

"I just want you to stop being like this. I've told you that it doesn't matter. Why don't we go back and play football, just you and me?"

"I don't care about football!" Rochy shouts. "Don't you understand? What does it matter to me if Real Madrid win La Liga or the Champions League? How does that make my life any better? I'll still be stuck here, with you, working in a factory. For ever."

I've never seen Rochy this angry before, and I don't

know what to say to calm him down. My eyes start filling with tears, but I'm determined not to cry in front of him.

"Do you know what I wanted to be when I was younger?" he asks.

I shrug weakly. My shoulders ache. "I don't know… a footballer?"

Rochy smiles, but it looks more like a grimace.

"No, Budi, not a footballer. I wanted to be an astronaut – someone who went out and discovered things, someone who changed the world. At school, I read every book I could find about space. My teacher said you need to be good at mathematics and physics to become an astronaut, so I took all the extra classes in those subjects that I could. I wanted to make my family proud, and to be able to send them money and nice things to make their lives more comfortable. But then my dad died, and I had to come and work at the factory, and I knew none of it would ever happen."

Rochy's face twists into another painful-looking smile, and he glances up at the narrow strip of sky above the alley.

"Do you know what's funny?"

I shake my head. I can't think of anything that's funny.

"I still want to be an astronaut. Only now I'm not

bothered about adventure or money or fame, or even providing my family with a better life. Now I want to be an astronaut so I can get as far away from this place – from you and everyone else in it – as possible." Rochy leans in and lowers his voice almost to a whisper. His hand is on the knife inside me. "I'm going to say this slowly so that you can understand it: I. Don't. Care. About. Football."

He straightens up and turns away. It's like I'm too full with all the bleeding inside, and the hot blood fills my eyes and spills over my cheeks.

"You're lying!" I shout, but Rochy keeps walking. "You must care about football! You have to!"

And suddenly I'm angry. Angry that Rochy is walking away from me. Angry that he doesn't care. Angry that I'm crying. My whole body tingles with rage. I clench my hands into fists and run after Rochy. I'm so angry that I don't know what to do when I catch up with him, so I just shove him in the back as hard as I can. He takes a couple of steps to steady himself and reels around. I close my eyes and throw myself at him, swinging my arms in a flurry of punches.

I open my eyes just before I hit the ground. Stones scratch against my bare chest. I can feel Rochy standing over me. As I try to get up he kneels on my back, pinning me among the litter of the alleyway. I try to lift my head, but Rochy pushes it into a gritty puddle. I remember too late how much bigger Rochy is. The air is being pressed from my lungs. It feels as though my ribcage is about to collapse.

"What's wrong with you?" he shouts, punching me in the side. "What don't you understand? I don't care about any of it and neither should you! Do you really think you make Kieran Wakefield's boots? Or that one day you'll visit the Bernabéu? Wake up, Budi!"

He punches me in the side again.

I'm bleeding. I know I'm bleeding.

"Do you really think we'll ever get out of this place? We're never getting out! Never!"

He punches me again.

Bleeding. Can taste it.

Can't breathe.

"You'll never become a professional footballer, just like I'll never become an astronaut! It's time to grow up, Budi – this is all there is! This is your life!"

Rochy punches me in the side one last time and gets off my back.

I don't move. I just lie in the dirt. The grit sticks to

my chest, my cheek. I can taste it on my tongue. Rochy stands over me, panting. He takes half a step towards me and I brace myself. But he doesn't kick me.

He just steps back.

Turns around.

Walks away.

I lie completely still, breathing in the salty, earthy smell of the wet ground. My ribcage hurts. When I get to my feet my body feels heavy and numb, like I've slept for a long time in an awkward position. I dust myself down and rub my side. I'm not crying any more.

I pick up my shirt and football and shuffle home, dragging my feet.

Kieran Wakefield could earn my yearly wage in the time it takes me to get home.

When I walk through the door Mum almost drops the cup of water she's holding up to Grandma's lips. Grandma must have had another coughing fit because her eyes are red and watery, and she scowls at the cup in front of her. She doesn't seem to notice that I'm here.

"Budi!" Mum says, her eyes wide. "What have you been doing?"

I look down at my aching, shirtless body. There is a big muddy stripe along my side. Rainwater drips from my fringe onto the floor. My shirt feels cold and heavy in my hand.

"You're absolutely filthy!" Mum says, setting the cup down on the table and coming over to me. "You've been out playing football, haven't you? What were you thinking? Have you cut yourself anywhere? Your clothes are soaked – and look at your boots! We can't afford to buy you a new pair if those get ruined."

My feet feel soggy and sandy inside my shoes. As I roll my foot to the side I notice that the upper is coming away from the sole.

"You know how tight money is at the moment, Budi, and the last thing we need is to be buying clothes to replace the ones you've ruined. You can't play football for ever, you know. You'll have to grow up one day."

"What about professional footballers?" I ask, tears coming to my eyes again. "They play football all the time. When I'm a professional footballer I'll get a new pair of boots every week."

"Stop being childish, Budi, and don't talk back to me like that."

"That's enough," Grandma says. "Bickering won't solve anything."

Mum takes a deep breath and sighs.

"Let's get you dry and into some clean clothes," she says. "Who knows how we'll pay for the medicine if you catch a fever. You'll be on rice porridge and water until you get better."

I get changed out of my damp clothes. My side starts to really hurt but I know nothing's broken, because I never break anything. I just bleed on the inside and no one sees.

There isn't anything for dinner because it's Friday, so I lie on my mattress instead. I unroll my poster but no matter how long I look at it I can't see anything new. I must have memorized every blade of grass and every colourful smudge in the crowd.

My finger moves in a continuous pattern, tracing the lines of Wakefield's autograph over and over again, and I know, without even thinking about it, that I will have to sell my poster to keep my family out of the slums.

I think of what I'd give just to be one of those smudges.

# DOUBLE TROUBLE

**R**ochy isn't at work the next day.

The foreman asks me where he is and I tell him that I don't know, because I don't. He tells me to tell Rochy that he's fired. I try to argue but the foreman ignores me. I try again and he strikes me with the *rotan*. While I'm still wincing against the pain, he turns around and waves to a girl on the other side of the factory. She hurries over and sits in Rochy's seat. She starts sewing.

Every few minutes I glance at the door in the hope that Rochy is just running late. After a caning and a week on the boxing section he might be allowed to keep his job. But Rochy doesn't turn up. No matter how many times I look at the door, it doesn't open.

Eventually I turn to the new girl and ask her who she

supports. If she's going to be sitting next to me from now on, I should probably find out what kind of person she is.

"What do you mean?" she says, staring at her machine.

"Which team do you support? Real Madrid, Manchester United…*Barcelona*?"

"I don't really like football," she says, placing the finished upper on a pile and starting a new one.

I can hardly believe it. This is a nightmare. Who doesn't like football? How am I supposed to sit next to someone who doesn't know the first thing about Real Madrid?

I am suddenly struck by a terrible thought.

"Do you know who Kieran Wakefield is?"

She turns her head to look at me.

"No. Should I?"

My mouth falls open. Does she live on another planet?

"It…it doesn't matter," I mumble.

I look at the door and cross my fingers.

Come on, Rochy. Come on.

But still he doesn't come.


After possibly the most boring day that anyone has ever worked, I walk home with my hands in my pockets. If my day had been a football match, it would have been a goalless draw. Not even a shot on target. Nil–nil.

The rain has stopped, but the sky is low with dark thunderclouds. I drag my feet, not wanting to get home too soon. Dad will still be gone. Mum will still be upset. Grandma will still be quiet. And this is the last time I'll walk home to my signed poster of Kieran Wakefield.

Cars and scooters crawl along beside me, pouring their fumes out into the air. They jostle for the tiniest spaces. They beep at nothing. I pick my way through the gaps, turning off the main road and into the maze of side streets. The washing lines that hang between the buildings are empty, like Real Madrid have lost the title. I wonder what will happen in the match tonight, but it doesn't really seem that important any more.

Maybe Rochy was right. Maybe it's time to wake up.

When I get home Mum is getting ready to visit the police station.

"I don't know if they'll let me speak to Elvis," she says, wrapping a scarf around her head, "but I've got to try. There's a tray of rice on the table for your dinner. Sorry there isn't anything else but until your father is released that's all we can really afford." Mum leans over and kisses me on the head. "Are you watching the football at Rochy's tonight?"

I nod, even though obviously I'm not.

"Good, it might help to take your mind off things." Mum steps across to the doorway, then changes her mind and comes back. She crouches down in front of me so that her eyes are lower than mine. "Everything will be okay, understand? This is just a bit of a rough patch but we'll get through it. We always do, don't we, Grandma?"

Grandma nods from her armchair. She smiles but she looks tired.

"That's right," she says. "Everything always works out in the end."

Mum stands up and leaves without another word. On the table there are two steel trays with a small mound of rice on each.

"You can have mine," Grandma says. "I'm not that hungry tonight."

"But you've always got an appetite, Grandma."

"I know," she says, sighing. "But not tonight. What I could really use is a cigarette, but I've only got a few left and I want to make them last."

I sit down and try to eat slowly, but it's all over in three mouthfuls. Then I slide Grandma's tray towards me.

"Are you sure, Grandma?" I ask.

"Go on," she says, her eyes closed, her head resting on her chest. "You're a growing boy. You need it."

"We could share it," I say.

But all I get in reply is a soft grunt. So I eat Grandma's dinner as well.

By the time I've finished Grandma is snoring quietly, so no one sees me leave with the poster.

There is a pawnbroker on the edge of the market who buys all kinds of things and sells them on to other people. He always has wads of cash folded around his fingers, so I know if anyone has the money to buy something rare and expensive it will be him.

The muddy ground between the market stalls is littered with vegetable peel and fruit rinds. The odd petal, from one of the flower stands, is trodden into the muck. Sellers sit on mats among sacks of pulses and spices, droning out their prices in a steady chant. The multicoloured canopies overhead hang dark and heavy with the weight of rain. I hear two women arguing with a trader over the price of a cut of meat. They say they won't pay that much for a dog. Dead, pink flesh is stacked up at the front of the stall, and blackened bodies hang from hooks around the edge. The spicy air is heavy with the smell of blood.

All around people shuffle through the mud, listening for the price of goods. I notice a group of dirty children about half my age slipping through the crowd, and I clutch my poster closer to my chest. When I reach the building at the far end of the market there are microwaves and ornaments and bits of clothing piled up on tables outside. The pawnbroker sits at the back of the dim room with his feet propped up on a box of coat hangers. The soles of his feet are black, and his vest hangs limply from his bony shoulders.

As I enter I have to duck because the shutter has only been raised halfway. The room is cool and gloomy, and a radio crackles in the corner. As I approach the man he scratches his scrawny arm and burps.

"What have you got for me?" he asks.

Very carefully, I unroll the poster and hold it up for him to see.

"I don't buy posters, kid. Go home."

"But it's signed," I say. "It's worth a lot of money."

"Ha! I don't think so. That's not a real autograph."

"Yes, it is, *Bapak*. I promise. There's even an eleven in the loop, see?"

"Look," he says, sitting forward and sorting through the roll of notes around his middle finger. "I don't have

216

time for whatever game it is you're playing. They print those things by the thousand. That signature will be in the same corner of every copy."

I feel tears coming to my eyes but I blink them away.

"You're lying! You just want me to believe it's fake so you can offer me a cheaper price!"

The man stops counting the notes and stands up.

"I don't want your stupid poster, kid! Now get out of here before I beat you!"

He reaches down for a coat hanger and I quickly duck under the shutter and make my way into the crowd. The tears come again but this time I let them roll down my cheeks. I lower my head and let myself be knocked from shoulder to shoulder, not caring as my poster is crumpled and torn by the press of bodies. A group of men stand by an electronics stall, laughing, and I feel my cheeks grow hot.

How could anyone be so stupid?

I fight against the crowd, desperate to escape. People raise their hands and shout as I force a path through the wall of bodies. Someone shoves me and I stumble, landing on my hands. A dirty, gnarled foot swings in my direction, and I have to scamper between two stalls to avoid it. I crawl behind a pile of sacks, dragging my poster along with me, before getting to my feet. My knees and hands are black with mud, but I keep going. I run down an alley – the dark, low sky like a roof above me – and I don't stop running until I'm out in the open by a busy road.

I double over, my muddy hands on my muddy knees, and breathe hard. The breath catches in my chest and I shudder. I cry properly, like a hungry baby. My whole body seems to shake. Tears blur my vision and I can feel strands of saliva dripping from my open mouth.

No one on the pavement stops. They walk by, quickening their pace to get past me. I wipe my forearm across my eyes and stare down at the ruined poster in my hands. Wakefield's pristine white kit is covered in mud. A corner has been ripped off. The autograph is unreadable among all the folds and crinkles.

And I can't help thinking, standing here in my fake boots, holding a fake poster – am I living a fake life, in a fake world?

My hands tighten around the poster, crumpling it even more, and I search for somewhere to throw it away. That's when I realize where I am, and why the congested road seems so familiar.

I'm standing outside the factory, closed for the night.

I remember what Rochy said about working at the

factory for ever. About waiting for something that's never going to happen. And as I look at the chained and padlocked door, dark clouds looming over the roof, it's hard to imagine ever escaping it.

I walk round the side of the factory to the big bins. Hauling one of the lids open, I pause before tossing the poster in. I'm about to drop the lid when I notice the homeless man curled up on a bed of cardboard inside. He must be drunk again because he doesn't stir. I close the lid and turn to leave.

But I stop. A man with long hair and grey rags shuffles towards one of the other bins. Just before he reaches it he glances over at me and raises the half-empty bottle in his hand.

"Monsoooooon!" he shouts, pointing at the sky. Then he lifts the lid and tumbles inside.

I look back at the bin in front of me. I grip the edge of the lid and ease it open, but I can't see anything. The darkening sky forces me to open it further for a better look. The man inside moves to cover his head but he's too slow. The face is unmistakable.

"U-Uncle?" I stammer.

The man lowers his hand, and I see the same dark eyes that stared at me from a newspaper page. But his expression isn't cold and fierce. His black eyebrows bunch in confusion, and his stubbly mouth hangs open, unsure what to say. He looks like a tired, grubby version of Dad.

"Uncle Aaron," I say, trying to sound familiar but just sounding scared. "It's me, Budi."

His face softens. He looks down at the crumpled poster on his lap, and after a moment's hesitation he scrambles to get out of the bin. I always imagined he would be stocky and strong, but as I help him out I can feel how thin he is through his torn prison clothes. He leans a hand on my shoulder as he stands, exhausted by the sudden exertion.

"Is it really you, Budi?" he says, staring hard into my eyes.

"Yes, Uncle," I say. The pressure on my shoulder grows, and I notice how unsteady he is. "Why don't we sit down for a moment?"

Uncle takes a long look around before agreeing, and we rest with our backs against the bin.

"You know," he says, "it's been a long time since anyone called me Uncle." He tries to smile. "Or Aaron, come to think of it."

"Why?" I ask. "What did they call you in…on…?" I struggle to find the right word.

"In prison?" he asks, offering another painful-looking smile. "On Nusa Kambangan?"

I nod. He says "Nusa Kambangan" the way I say "Barcelona".

"They called me whatever they wanted to call me. But officially I was known as 9875B."

He closes his eyes and takes a deep breath in through his nose.

"Isn't it wonderful?" he asks. When he opens his eyes again I notice they are lined with tears. "Take a deep breath and tell me it isn't the sweetest thing."

I do as I'm told. My nostrils fill with the smell of petrol and rained-on tarmac. I cough a little bit.

"It's wonderful," I say.

When I look at Uncle again he is staring at me with a faint smile on his face, shaking his head.

"I can't believe how much you've grown," he says. "You must be at least eleven by now."

"I turned twelve last week."

He lets out a low whistle. "Has it really been that long?" he asks, although he seems to be asking someone else. We sit in silence for a few minutes, watching the storm clouds deepen and darken. Soon it will be night.

"I'm guessing you're not a Real Madrid fan?" Uncle

asks, jabbing a thumb over his shoulder towards the bin.

For a moment I don't know what he's talking about, but then I remember my poster.

"No, I am," I say. "They're the greatest team in the world. One day I'm going to play for them."

I feel stupid as soon as I've said it, but my uncle raises his eyebrows in interest.

"Is that so?"

"Well, the first step is getting into the academy. If I could afford to play there I might get spotted. But it's impossible without sponsorship, and I don't know if I'm good enough."

He smiles. "So why are you canning a poster of that pretty boy if you're such a big fan?"

I look at my boots. My fake boots.

"It's ruined," I say.

Uncle nods. He seems to understand. "Does Ríos still play for Real Madrid? He was a magician."

Rochy told me all about Ríos – one of the best footballers who ever lived. His nickname was Ríos "*El Dios*" – the God. He won every trophy going and scored hundreds of goals for Real Madrid. Nobody liked to play against him because he was unstoppable. A bit like Kieran Wakefield really.

But he retired. Ages ago. When I was about four.

"No," I say. "Kieran Wakefield is their best player now."

My uncle shakes his head. "Never heard of him."

"What? You must have! He's the one on the poster. What about León Belmonte?"

Uncle shakes his head again. "Unfortunately I didn't get to watch much football on the inside."

I frown, picking at the loose sole of my shoe.

"Uncle," I say. "How long were you inside for?"

"A long time. Years and years. Too many to count."

He watches as I tighten my shoe. The three little cuts on my fingertip bleed into the laces.

"When did you do that?" he asks, nodding at my injury.

"About a week ago."

He looks into my face. "So you've got the family curse too?"

Uncle rolls up his sleeve and shows me a graze on his forearm that's surrounded by a purple bruise. The blood still looks wet.

"We used to get through a tin of coconut butter a week, Elvis and I, when we were boys. It's a dangerous business, being a brother."

He turns away again, touching the cut on his arm.

"It seems like a different life," he says. "Looking back."

For a moment I think he's going to say something else, but instead he unrolls his sleeve and stares at the ground between his feet. It starts to rain. I think about Dad, and the choice the Dragon gave to Grandma.

"What are you going to do?" I ask. "I mean, there are people out hunting for you. You're on the front pages of the newspapers. Surely you can't run for ever."

"I know, and I don't intend to keep running. I just want to see my family again – to make things right. I knew it wouldn't be long before they finished me on that island, and I didn't want to die without saying goodbye. I don't even know whether my mother is still alive."

"She's fine," I say, struggling to concentrate on Uncle's words. "She's indestructible."

Uncle laughs, but all I can hear is Grandma's voice repeating the same sentence.

*You can't expect a mother to sacrifice one son to save another.*

Uncle looks in both directions to check we're still alone, but I doubt he can see very far in the darkness.

"I don't expect you to help me, Budi, but if you could take me to your parents, just so I can talk to them. Then I promise to disappear. For good."

Then it's the Dragon's voice, calm and insistent in my head.

*If Aaron were to co-operate in a little export project I've been working on, we could help keep him out of prison for good, couldn't we, brother?*

And then I realize that Grandma shouldn't be made to choose between her sons. I desperately try to think of another way, but I can't escape the voice in my head.

My voice.

*The decision is yours, Budi. You must make the choice.*

"Okay," I say. "I'll take you."

"Really? You'd do that for me?"

I look at my feet. "Yes."

"Thank you!" Uncle says, drawing me into a hug. He holds me so tightly that he squeezes a tear to my eye. I quickly wipe it away.

"But you can't just walk through the streets," I say. "Someone might recognize you. If you wait here I'll bring somebody to fetch you."

"How long will you be?"

"Not long."

Uncle clambers back into the bin and I set off, wandering the streets until I find what I'm looking for. I was right – it doesn't take long. I approach the police car sitting by the kerb and knock on the glass.

The window rolls down and a young policeman sticks his head out.

"What do you want?" he asks.

"I need the Chief Inspector."

"Oh yeah? And what makes you think he'll come out in the rain for some street kid?"

"Because I've found something the Dragon has been looking for. And unless you want to upset the Dragon, I suggest you do as I say."

The policeman looks at me as though I've just pulled the pin from a hand grenade.

Then he scrambles for his walkie-talkie and calls it in.

# THE IMPOSSIBLE DREAM

The Chief Inspector is not alone. He's brought two officers with him, and all three of them squint into the rain.

"Where is he?" the Chief Inspector asks.

"Before I tell you I need you to promise not to hurt him—"

The Chief Inspector slaps me across the face.

"I'll hurt who I like," he says. "Now, where is he?"

"He doesn't know you're coming, so it will be better if I talk to him."

I get another slap.

"I'm warning you! You either tell us where he is or you can share a cell with your *kurang ajar* father."

I rub my cheek.

"Follow me."

We walk around to the side of the factory. The two officers draw their revolvers and hold them out in front. Just like in the movies. Except the real bad guy isn't the one hiding in the bin. He's the one with his hand on my shoulder, keeping me in front like a human shield.

"If this is a trap I'll break your neck before you can scream," the Chief Inspector mutters, digging his fingers into the soft muscle around my spine.

I come to a stop.

"Which one?" he hisses.

I point to the right bin.

"Could be a trap, sir," one of the officers says. "There could be a lot of firepower in the rest of those bins. Should I call for backup?"

The Chief Inspector waves the officers forward with his free hand.

"We don't need backup. Just get the bin open!"

The officers creep forward, exchanging glances every few steps. When they reach the bin they stand on either side and raise their guns to the lid. One of them places a hand on the edge as they count down.

"*Tiga…dua…satu…*"

The lid swings open and the two officers point their

guns into the bin. They bark orders, shouting to be heard against the rain. Uncle emerges with his hands up, looking bewildered. Then he sees me standing beside the Chief Inspector and his face falls. The Chief Inspector's hand rests on my shoulder, and I glance up to see a wide, ugly smile.

"Get the cuffs on him!" he shouts.

Uncle is dragged onto the wet ground and forced to place his hands behind his back. He manages to twist his neck to look at me. The Chief Inspector pats me on the shoulder.

"Good boy," he says. "You'll go far in this world."

When he says that my heart feels like it's been kicked. Hard. Like a goal-line clearance in the ninetieth minute.

Uncle is lifted to his feet and marched to the Chief Inspector's car. He doesn't look at me as he passes.

"Put him in the back!" the Chief Inspector says. "And not a word of this to anyone!"

He reaches into his pocket and splits a bundle of notes between the two officers. They get into a separate car and pull away from the roadside.

"Little Lazaro," the Chief Inspector says, grinning. "Why don't you sit in the front with me, like a real policeman?"

He opens the passenger door and I slump onto the seat. I'm not tall enough to see Uncle's reflection in the mirror, and for once I'm grateful for being small. I stare through the rain-speckled windscreen as the Chief Inspector climbs in and steps on the accelerator.

It's the first time I've ever been in a car. It's one of the worst experiences of my life.

Even though the journey is over in a couple of minutes it feels like we drive for miles and miles. The wiper things thrash from side to side but the screen is never clear. I wish my uncle would say something, anything. But he doesn't. The silence gets so big I worry the windows are going to shatter under the pressure. I sink lower in my seat.

The side streets leading to the Dragon's house are too narrow for the police car so we get out and walk. The Chief Inspector holds onto Uncle's handcuffs, steering him through the dark alleyways. I trail behind, dragging my feet.

We climb the steps to the first floor and find the Dragon sitting in near darkness. He smiles at the sight of my uncle, and the reddish *sirih*-spit between his teeth looks black in the gloom. His jewellery catches the yellow light thrown from a lamp, making the gold chains around his neck look fake and tarnished. As he lifts his feet from the low table, he scatters loose notes onto the floor but doesn't seem to notice. I've never seen the Dragon stand up to greet anyone, but he hauls himself out of his chair and holds Uncle by the shoulders.

"Aaron," he says, still grinning. "It's a pleasure to meet you." Then he turns to the Chief Inspector and frowns. "Why is this hero handcuffed like a petty thief? The man is our guest. Untie him!"

"I thought it best, brother. He has a reputation, you know."

"Reputation?" The Dragon scowls. "Yes, I know. He has a reputation for escaping from a high-security prison! What use do you think those bracelets are going to be?"

The Dragon spits on the floor in his brother's direction. The Chief Inspector pulls a face but shuffles over and unlocks the handcuffs.

"How did you find him anyway?" the Dragon asks, returning to his seat. "Did the old woman turn him in?"

"No, it was the boy."

The Dragon notices me for the first time. "You're a real bad man, Little Lazaro. Not many people could betray their own family. It's not easy, I know. I'm sure you heard the rumour about one of my brothers who lost his fingers in an accident."

The Chief Inspector shuffles uncomfortably. My uncle doesn't flinch. I look at the floor.

"Shall I make a call to the station?" the Chief Inspector says, changing the subject. "Release the boy's father?"

The Dragon waves a hand. For the first time since he was arrested, Uncle glances across at me.

"Let's see whether Aaron is willing to demonstrate a bit of family loyalty first." The Dragon interlocks his fingers into one huge fist, the heavy rings jostling against each other for space. "You see, Aaron, you have arrived at a rather traumatic time for your family. Your brother, Elvis, is currently being questioned for information about your whereabouts. He says he doesn't know anything."

"He doesn't," Uncle says through gritted teeth.

"Well, that's what the Chief Inspector needs to be sure of before he can release him. In the meantime, Elvis's family – *your* family – are struggling to pay the rent, and it won't be long until your mother, sister-in-law and nephew are fighting for a shack in the slums." The Dragon looks at me and smirks. "Although maybe you feel some of them might deserve it."

Uncle takes a deep breath and fixes the Dragon with his dark eyes.

"So what do you want?"

"I want you to help me. Right now, there is a container truck sitting outside the factory where your nephew works. It's full of football boots – hundreds and hundreds of pairs. We're talking billions of rupiah. And it will sit there all day tomorrow and all night before someone drives it to the port on Monday morning."

The Dragon pauses to fire a watery jet of spit over his shoulder.

"Now, this isn't a Jakarta street stall we want to rob. This container belongs to some rich Americans, and when they find out what's happened they won't just let it slide. My brother won't be any protection against a foreign investigation. So we need someone who can break into the truck without leaving a trail. Someone like you, Aaron."

Uncle shakes his head. "It can't be done," he says.

The Dragon's eyes widen. I should have warned Uncle that nobody crosses the Dragon unless they want to be chewed up and spat out.

"Of course it can be done. Your career is legendary – people still can't believe some of the jobs you pulled."

"I got caught, didn't I?"

"And you escaped."

Uncle shakes his head again.

"It won't work. If no one discovered what had happened until a few weeks later, after the container arrived at its destination, you might have a chance. But the container won't even make it out of the port."

"Why not?" asks the Chief Inspector.

Uncle glances over his shoulder but responds to the Dragon.

"Because they weigh each container to make sure it's right. If the weight is too far out, they open it up and check what's inside."

The Dragon grins, and *sirih*-spit bubbles around his teeth.

"We won't just be taking things out, we'll be putting something back in."

Uncle frowns. "Like what?"

"People."

"People?" I blurt out, but the Dragon ignores me.

"For every pallet we remove, we'll replace it with someone who has paid to get out of this place." The Dragon looks at me. "You might want to consider it too, Little Lazaro. If you've got a million rupiah to spare I'll book you a space."

Uncle rubs a hand across his face.

"And if I help you my brother will be released?"

"Of course," the Dragon says.

"And then what? Your brother hands me in and gets a medal?"

The Dragon and the Chief Inspector exchange a glance.

"We can keep you out of prison," the Dragon says, sitting forward in his chair. "Do this for us and we'll give you a new life. A new start, for you and your family."

"And I'm supposed to just take your word for it?" Uncle says, looking from the Dragon to the Chief Inspector and back again. "Not that it matters. It's not like I have a choice." Then he looks at me. "I came here to make things right with my family, and if this is what it takes then that's what I'll do."

The Dragon smacks his hand down on the arm of the chair.

"Then it's settled! You can stay here tonight. We'll get you a change of clothes and something to eat. Do you want me to send for anything else, brother?"

Uncle stares at the Dragon. "I just want a meal and a bed, that's all."

"We'll send someone out for food. You can have

anything you want." The Dragon waves his hand at me. "Why don't you go home, Little Lazaro? And remember to keep what you've heard to yourself. Otherwise you'll end up in a cell with your father and your uncle, while the women in your family work for me."

My hands curl into fists. I want to beat the Dragon's smug expression into his skull. But I notice that Uncle is looking at me, and the stillness in his eyes calms me down.

"It's okay, Budi," he says. "Go home now."

I can't believe how much he looks like Dad, and suddenly it doesn't feel as though we've been kept apart for years and years. It feels as though he's been looking after me all along.

"We'll call for you tomorrow evening," the Dragon says, twisting one of his rings around his finger. "You know the factory compound as well as anyone. We might need you."

The Chief Inspector grips my arm and shoves me out of the room. He follows me down the stairs but stops at the entrance, not wanting to step into the rain. I glance back as I cross the square and he spits into the dirt.

As soon as I turn the corner I run, not stopping until I reach the apartment. Grandma is asleep in the darkness, her breathing slow and shallow. I creep towards my room, glad that I don't have to talk to anyone, and curl up on my mattress.

I hear Mum come home a while later. She wakes Grandma and says that she waited for hours at the police station but they wouldn't let her speak to Dad. Grandma tells her not to worry. She tells her that everything will be all right, but I don't know whether I believe her. A cold tear runs across my cheek and soaks into the mattress. It's the first time I've ever thought Grandma might be lying.

Mum must go to bed soon after, because gradually everything grows quiet except for the pattering of raindrops outside.

Grandma coughs in the next room and I decide to get up. The room is completely black except for the glowing orange tip of Grandma's cigarette.

"Are you okay, Grandma?" I ask. "Can I get you some water?"

"That's very kind, Budi, but I'm fine, thank you."

The orange glow flares up to an angry red, then almost disappears completely.

"Would you like me to tell you a story?" she asks.

I walk over and sit cross-legged on the threadbare patch by her chair. She coughs quietly, like she's growling.

"What kind of story would you like?" she says.

"I don't mind. How about your favourite?"

"My favourite? Well, let me see. That's a tough one. Did I ever tell you the story about the swimmer?"

"No. Is it your favourite?"

"I should say so."

"Then why haven't you told it before?"

Grandma takes one last drag on her cigarette and stubs it out.

"Because I wanted to save the best for last," she says.

"You haven't got any more stories to tell?" I ask.

"No, this is the last one."

I never thought Grandma would run out of stories.

"Now then," she says, "the story goes that there was a boy who lived on a remote island—"

"Is this the one with the big coconut tree? Because you've told me that one already."

"No, that's about a different boy on a different island. It's a completely different story altogether. Now, where was I? Oh yes, there was once a boy who lived on a remote island."

"What was his name?"

"His name was Budi."

"No, it wasn't! You're making this up."

"Are you calling me a liar, young man? I'll have you

know this story has been told for generations, and I doubt anyone has interrupted its telling as much as you have. And it's true that the boy was called Budi."

"But that's my name."

"I know – you were named after him."

"Really? I didn't know that."

"Well, you were. I suggested the name to your parents when you were born, and they asked, 'Why Budi?' They were sceptical, you see. After all, I did name your father Elvis." She laughs, but it soon turns into another hacking cough. "Anyway, after I told your parents this story they thought it was a wonderful name, and they agreed to call you Budi."

"So how does the story go?"

"As I was saying, there was once a boy – named Budi – who lived on a remote island. Life on this island was very tough, and it was often a struggle just to get by. They didn't even have the tools or resources to build boats, so they had to fish by wading into the shallows with spears. It was very primitive, but everyone worked together and kept each other happy, even when the storms came or they didn't have much to eat.

"None of the surrounding islands thought much of Budi's island. They said it was too small and rocky and exposed – life was too harsh – so they never visited. But occasionally bad weather would force fishermen from other islands onto the shore, and for a few hours Budi and his family would hear stories about how much better life was across the water. No matter how much Budi pleaded with the fishermen, they never allowed him to journey back to these distant paradises in their boats. He was well and truly marooned."

Grandma stops, and after a while I begin to think she might have fallen asleep. Then I hear a rattling sound, and all of a sudden a flame bursts into life, throwing white light onto her face. It makes her look very pale, and all the little wrinkles lengthen and multiply as she sucks on the end of a new cigarette. She shakes her hand and the match goes out.

"What happened next, Grandma? Did he get off the island?"

"All in good time, there's no rush. One night, there was a terrible storm that felled a lot of the trees the islanders relied on for food and shelter. When the skies finally cleared, things were worse than ever. That's when Budi decided that he had to get off the island."

"But how? They didn't have any boats, remember?"

"I know, and Budi knew this as well as anybody. But

there's one thing I haven't mentioned yet – Budi loved to swim. He went out into the ocean every day, not just to fish, but to swim between the waves. He used to circle the island – which admittedly wasn't very far – and dive underwater to see how long he could hold his breath. The only problem was that the nearest island was little more than a smudge on the horizon, and that's a long way even for a good swimmer. Still, times were very tough on the island, and Budi knew he had to do something. So the day after the storm, just after sunrise, Budi announced that he would swim to the next island.

"As you might imagine, the islanders were full of discouragement. 'What about the sharks and the jellyfish?' one of them asked. 'The currents will drag you out to sea,' another said. 'It's too far,' they all agreed. Of course, Budi knew this. He knew how great the dangers were, but to do nothing might prove equally perilous. Indeed, the only people who supported his decision were his family and friends."

"But weren't they worried about him? And wouldn't they be sad if he went?"

"Of course, but they knew it was for the best and so they were happy to see him go, in a sad way. They watched him wade out into the ocean and followed him for as long as possible. Soon he was just a speck between the waves. Then they lost sight of him altogether.

"You see, sometimes you have to go it alone. Miles away from land with aching arms and tired legs, Budi must have felt miserable, lonely and afraid. But I'm sure he also knew that even during times of desperate isolation you are never truly alone. There is always someone rooting for you, always someone who believes. And he knew that if he never stopped kicking he would get there in the end.

"You must never give up, Budi. You must keep kicking. I believe in you."

Grandma falls silent, and in between drags I hear her heavy breathing.

"What happened next?" I ask quietly. "Did he make it?"

"What do you think?"

"I'm not sure. I hope so."

The glowing orange tip dances in the darkness as Grandma adjusts her position.

"You fell out with your friend, didn't you?"

"How do you know that?"

"There isn't much that gets past an old lady like me. Do you want to talk about it?"

"Not really." I rub my side where Rochy punched me

and suddenly realize that I *do* want to talk about it, more than anything. "Rochy said that I'll never become a professional footballer. And that I'll never see Kieran Wakefield play at the Bernabéu. He pinned me to the ground and punched me as well."

Even though it's Grandma, and even though I know she can't see me, I feel ashamed.

"That's not very nice of him. I thought Rochy was a friendly boy."

"He is. At least, I thought he was."

"I'm sure he didn't mean to hurt you. People say and do lots of things they don't mean when they're angry or upset, but you mustn't listen to them. Don't let anybody tell you something is impossible. Impossible is nothing."

Grandma's cigarette crackles and glows as she takes another drag.

"I'm sure you won't stay enemies for long. Everything will be back to normal again soon. Now, it's very late. I think maybe you should go to bed."

"Just one more thing, Grandma, and then I'll go, I promise."

"Okay, what is it?"

I desperately want to tell her that her son is in hiding just around the corner. That she doesn't need to worry about choosing between her children because I've done it for her. That we're on the verge of a new life together, the five of us. But then I remember the Dragon's warning, about how he would ruin us all if I mentioned anything, and change my mind.

Sometimes, sharing is the selfish thing to do.

"Did you ever get to meet Elvis?" I ask.

Grandma chuckles. "Oh, I wondered what you were going to ask me then."

"But did you?"

Grandma sighs. "Yes, just once. It was very memorable. But that's another story for another time."

"I thought you didn't have any stories left to tell?"

Grandma chuckles again. "You don't miss anything, do you? Now, give me a hug before you go."

I stand up and Grandma squeezes me tightly. I pick my way through the darkness to my bedroom, but as I reach the door Grandma stops me.

"Budi," she says. "No matter what happens, keep kicking."

I look back, but all I can see is the glowing tip of her cigarette.

"Goodnight, Grandma."

"Goodnight."

# HOUSE OF SAND

I'm lying on a beach. My whole body aches. Waves crash onto the shore with such force I can feel them through the sand. The vibrations hurt my tired muscles. I know that if I'm lying on a beach I must have made it. I can't be dead or drowned because I can feel the wind scattering sand over my face. I keep my eyes closed.

The pain in my limbs is almost enjoyable. It means I kept kicking. I'm not dead yet.

Another wave folds onto the shore. It must be a big one because I sink further into the sand. Little grains scurry across my shoulders like insects. I try to pull myself up but I'm too heavy, and the sand is too loose. I start to panic.

Someone calls my name, and I really panic. If someone

knows my name it means I didn't make it. I must have passed out and been washed up on the same island I swam from. And that's almost worse than being dead. The voice comes again, and another wave crashes in. It must be really big – tsunami big – because I feel like I'm falling through the sand with the impact of it. The sand rushes over my face, filling up my ears and nose and mouth. I know that if I don't open my eyes and get out I will die. But I just can't find the surface.

My voice is called again. It sounds strange through the sand. Someone reaches through the grains and pulls me up. But I thrash around. I don't want to face the wave. It's too big. It's too strong. It will sweep me away.

"Budi! Wake up! We need to get out!"

I open my eyes and immediately scrunch them shut against the grit. It's raining dust from the ceiling.

"Stop shaking me!" I say. "I'm awake!"

"Budi!"

It's Mum's voice, but not like I've ever heard it before. And then I notice another sound. A rumbling. Near and loud and growing. Like the world is hurting.

I wipe a hand over my face and the little grains grate against my skin. Shielding my eyes from the dusty light, I look up. The crack in the ceiling spreads in every direction and zigzags down the walls, like a giant is tearing the room apart. Mum grabs my arm and I scramble out of bed.

I stumble on the shaking ground. The earth lurches, throwing me onto my hands and knees. From outside I hear the sound of shrieking. There is a crunching, booming sound, and moments later a cloud of dust billows through the window.

"Under the table!" Mum shouts, trying to lift me to my feet.

"What about Grandma?" I ask, fighting my way towards her armchair.

"Leave me!" Grandma shouts. "Get under the table!"

I try to help her up, but she pushes me away with such desperate strength that I end up on my knees again, crawling under the table. Mum puts her arm around me and pulls me close, protecting me with her body. From where we hide I can see Grandma sitting with her hands folded on her lap, her head bowed, her eyes closed. I know Grandma hates earthquakes from the time Grandpa died. I hope she isn't as scared as me. I hope she remembers that Dad is in the strongest building in Jakarta. I hope she remembers that she's indestructible.

Rochy told me about earthquakes once. He said

they've got nothing to do with the world being hungry (like I thought), or Allah being angry (like Uston said). Rochy said that deep underground the world is made up of huge rocky plates, and all these plates are moving. They only move a tiny bit at a time, but sometimes they get stuck and the pressure builds up. Then one day, like today, something gives and they do years and years of moving in one go. I told him that I didn't think such tiny movements could result in something as big as an earthquake, but he swore it was true. And I think I believe him now.

Finally, the shaking stops. I hear the last few pieces of plaster drop onto the floor. Mum makes me wait beneath the table in case there is an aftershock. She rushes over to Grandma and wipes the dust from her hair and clothes. Grandma coughs, growling as she tries to clear the dust from her throat.

"I'm fine," she says, both hands pressed to her chest. "It's over now."

Grandma's eyes begin to water, and the squiggly vein stands out on her forehead. Mum goes to fetch her a drink, and as she moves I notice the building on the opposite side of the street through the window. I tilt my head to make it straight, but it's still not right.

I crawl out from under the table. Mum says something but I don't hear it. I can't take my eyes off the window. Shuffling across the room, I step outside.

The apartment block opposite – the one that's made of the wrong sort of concrete – is half the height it used to be. It looks like a dog that's folded its legs beneath itself. The lower floors have crumpled into one another, and the rest of the building leans towards the ground.

I step up onto a chunk of concrete in the middle of the road. The morning is already hot, but the air is so thick with dust that I can't see the sun. Around me, groups of people cling to each other, wailing at the sight of the destroyed building. Their clothes are white and chalky, their faces grey and smudged. They look like ghosts.

Somehow my apartment block is still standing. Big chunks have fallen from every building for as far as I can see. Each moment brings another person staggering out into the street, until soon the space in front of me is crowded with people trying to find relatives and friends. Their feet kick up clouds of dust. My mouth feels like a desert. Among the crying and shrieking I hear urgent voices – angry voices – but I can't tell what they're saying.

I saw a war film once. At the end, a group of planes flew over a town and dropped bombs on the houses. They weren't even the houses of soldiers. It was just families. Old people, grown-ups, children, babies. The bombs kept falling and the town kept getting smashed to pieces. And all the time there was this music playing, like the music they always play at the end of films when the good guys finally start winning. Except the good guys weren't winning. It was just people being bombed for no reason and left to pick up the pieces. And their streets looked like mine does now.

I suddenly think of Rochy – his crumbling room near the slums – and I jump down from the concrete boulder, turning back to my apartment. Mum still has her arm around Grandma, holding a cup of water to her dusty lips. Grandma isn't drinking. I'm out of breath, even though I haven't run anywhere.

"Rochy," I manage to say. "I have to check...I have to know."

"No," Mum says, standing up. "It's not safe."

But Grandma waves a hand.

Telling me to go.

Telling Mum to let me go.

And Mum knows she's right. She puts her hands on her hips and hangs her head.

"Just..."

She waves a hand like Grandma.

And I go. I push my way through the crowd of ghosts. Fallen air-conditioning units and shop signs and rubble block the narrow side streets, so I head towards the main road. I race along the pavement, hurdling over debris and weaving between toppled scooters. Among all the chaos and destruction I catch a glimpse of the factory, still standing as though nothing has happened.

I turn into the maze of streets that leads to Rochy's apartment. The buildings have slumped against each other, spilling chunks of concrete and plaster into the narrow lanes. There is a thin track through the wreckage, but as I get closer to the slums I have to climb over mounds of debris just to keep moving. Eventually I reach Rochy's street. I clamber over a hill of rubble and skid to a halt.

I don't stop because my legs are burning. I don't stop because my lungs feel raw. I don't stop because the cuts on my fingertip and knee are dripping blood.

I stop because there aren't any buildings in front of me.

I stop because there aren't any people in front of me.

I stop because I don't know if I can go on.

And then I notice someone standing between the mounds of twisted metal and broken concrete. He is the same colour as the dusty mess around him, and as I get closer I notice the pale number seven hanging off the back of his shirt.

Rochy doesn't turn to look at me when I reach his side. He just stares at the spot where his home used to be. A dark stripe cuts through the dust on each cheek like war paint. I think I must look the same.

I reach out and hold Rochy's hand.

"I just stepped outside," he whispers. "I was on my way to the dump. I didn't know...I didn't know this would happen."

I squeeze his hand, and I hear the soft patter of blood as my fingertip leaks onto the ground.

We stand here for a long time. We don't move, even when the rain comes to wash us clean. My legs don't ache. My shoulders don't burn. You only notice the thing that hurts the most, and in my chest there's a continuous plummeting, like my heart is sinking in a deep, cold ocean. Like someone is driving the knife in deeper and deeper. Always twisting, always pushing. Never finding the bottom. I hold Rochy's hand for so long it feels as though we've merged. When a muscle twitches I can't tell who it belongs to. When my finger bleeds, it bleeds with Rochy's blood.

"I'm sorry," he says eventually.

I understand without asking.

"I'm sorry too."

The sky begins to darken. Sirens get louder without getting closer. People drift by, picking through the wreckage. Digging.

"We should go," I say. "Come home with me."

Rochy shakes his head. Rain drips from his nose and chin. His shirt isn't a faded pink any more. It's the blood-red colour it should be.

"I don't want to leave," he says. "I can't."

I look into his face, and I wonder if he'll ever be able to stop crying. Or will he just stand here for ever, seeping into the rubble? Our hands separate, and I take a step towards home. But I turn back before leaving.

"Whenever you're ready," I say. "We'll be waiting for you."

Then I go, trudging through muddy streets and over mounds of broken buildings. In some places people search for survivors. In others they search for things they can eat or burn or sell. Makeshift shelters spring up in the gaps between gaps.

When I get home Mum is sitting at the table, biting her nails and staring at the wall. She doesn't notice me until I speak.

"Mum," I say.

Then I notice the empty armchair.

"Where's Grandma?"

"Oh, Budi," Mum says, and in a flash she's up and hugging me to her chest. She doesn't even seem to notice that I'm soaked through, that I'm bleeding. Bleeding on the outside, bleeding on the inside. "I don't know how to tell you. She's gone. Grandma's gone. We've lost her."

I manage to prise myself away and look up into Mum's eyes. They're red and swollen.

"She can't have gone far," I say. "She can hardly walk. And she falls asleep too often. Have you checked the street?"

"No, Budi—"

"That's where we should look first. I'll go now."

"No, Budi," Mum says, catching my arm as I turn to leave.

When I look back, Mum is properly crying. Like she's hurt.

"What's the matter?" I ask.

"She's gone, Budi," Mum sobs. "Grandma's dead."

"But..."

But Grandma is indestructible. She's immune to venom. Once she fell out of a third-storey window and survived without a scratch.

Mum sits down in Grandma's armchair. It's a very strange thing to see. She doesn't fit properly among the cushions. I look down and realize a puddle is forming around my feet. My finger drips blood onto the rug.

"But she can't be," I say.

That's when the room goes blurry, like I'm looking at everything at the bottom of a stream. A stream that rushes around me, taking everything with it: the scattered cigarette butts, the rug, Grandma's chair with Mum still sitting in it. Soon I can't even see my feet, my legs, my waist. It feels as though I'm being swept away. Submerged. Drowning. And there's nothing I can do. Nothing to hold on to.

And so I let go.

# THERE GOES MY EVERYTHING

"I have to tell your father," Mum says.

My eyes start to refocus. Mum's hand rests on my shoulder. She looks at me as though I've just woken up.

"Then I'm going to the hospital. To say goodbye. Do you want to come with me?"

"No," I mumble. "I'll stay here."

It's almost as though if I don't say goodbye, Grandma can't leave. If I don't see her, no one can prove that she's... no one can prove anything and it will never become real.

"Are you sure?" Mum asks. "I don't like the thought of you being here on your own like this."

"I'm okay," I say. "I'm sure."

She squeezes my shoulder and wipes a tear from her cheek.

"Okay," she says, straightening up. "I'll be back as soon as I can."

She closes her eyes and takes a deep breath. Then she steps out into the night.

I sit on the bald rug, picking at the tassels. There is still the smell of cigarette smoke in the air, the shape of Grandma in the cushions. Sitting in the gloom, I trick my ears into hearing her voice, my eyes into seeing the glowing tip of a cigarette. But it doesn't last.

A movement by the door makes me look up, and against the darkness of the street is an even darker silhouette.

"Little Lazaro," the voice says, "it's time to settle a debt."

The Dragon steps through the doorway and leans against the wall. His wet skin glistens, and his *sirih*-stained teeth look black when he smiles.

"Nobody saw this earthquake coming," he says, running a stubby finger along a crack in the wall. "Do you think I can still get the homeless to pay rent? Ha! It's just as well I've moved into other lines of business."

My hands clench into fists.

"I don't want to help you any more."

He frowns. "What was that? You want your father to

**257**

rot in a cell for the rest of his life? You want your mother to live in the slums? Is that what you really want, Little Lazaro?"

I look at the empty armchair and let out a long, slow breath. My hands relax.

"No, *Bapak*."

"Then get up and follow me."

The Dragon spits at me, his red saliva spattering the rug and mixing with my blood.

"Yes, *Bapak*."

I get to my feet and walk towards the door. But as I pass the Dragon, he grabs me by the shirt and leans in so close I can see the little red veins in his bloodshot eyes. He reaches down to his belt and draws something up to the side of my face.

A knife.

"Now, listen to me very carefully. My brother told me that while your father was being interrogated, he revealed a little family secret. It seems you all suffer from the same weakness." The Dragon moves the blade closer to my face. It flashes in the dim light. "The tiniest cut and it could all be over."

I want to tell him that it doesn't work like that. That it's bleeding on the inside that counts. That I'm bleeding on the inside already. But then the Dragon snatches my hand and lifts it up between our faces. He squeezes my finger until blood oozes from the three cuts.

"I suggest you are very careful tonight. You wouldn't want to be the cause of a family tragedy, would you?"

When I don't reply the Dragon squeezes my finger again. I wince as fresh blood dribbles down to my palm.

"No, *Bapak*."

"Good boy." He lets go of my hand and tucks the knife into his belt. "Now, let's not keep your uncle waiting any longer."

The Dragon shoves me out into the rain and we pick our way through the rubble. Little streams of dirty water flow in the spaces between broken concrete. As the Dragon approaches, people fade into the shadows and disappear between ruined buildings. It feels as though we're walking through a ghost town.

We reach a car just off the main road and the Dragon tells me to get in the back. Uncle sits on the backseat, clutching a rucksack on his lap. He's wearing a pair of gloves, the plastic ones I've seen doctors wear when Kieran Wakefield needs treatment. Uncle smiles at me but I have to look away, out of the window. I thought I was doing the right thing by making Grandma's choice for her, but now Uncle will never see his mother again. And it's all my fault.

Raindrops streak across the window as one of the Dragon's thugs drives us to the factory. Every so often the Dragon glances over his shoulder at us, but no one says anything. The only sound is the whining of the wiper things as they try to clear the screen, and the thudding of fat raindrops on the roof. Every few seconds a scooter splashes by, and the rain trails on the window glow white and flash red as it passes.

We pull in around the back of the factory, parking just out of sight of the gates. The engine is cut, the wipers stop mid-thrash, and the dying headlights plunge us into darkness. Raindrops rattle off the roof and bonnet like bullets. The Dragon twists around in his seat and checks his wristwatch.

"Give us the signal when you're in the compound," he says. "The van will be here any minute. Take your nephew with you."

"Can't Budi wait here?" Uncle says. "I'm used to working on my own. He doesn't need to come."

The Dragon shakes his head. "Take him with you – we might need him. He can carry your bag if nothing else."

Uncle glances at me and we climb out of the car.

The rain falls so hard that my face and arms sting. We jog through a long puddle towards the chained gates and Uncle quickly glances over each shoulder to check we're not being watched. Then he digs into the rucksack and takes out some tools.

"Put these on," he says, snapping off his gloves and handing them to me. "The last thing we need is for all this to be traced back to you."

"But what about you?"

Uncle smiles. "I think I'm in trouble either way."

I pull them on, struggling to get the stretchy plastic over my wet hands.

"Point this at the padlock," he says, clicking a torch on and passing it to me.

I do as I'm told and watch as his fingers fiddle with the lock. I never thought you could actually pick a lock with a pin – I just thought it was something they did in the movies. But within a few seconds the padlock pops open, and Uncle unravels the chains that hold the gates together. He crouches down and works the bolt out of the ground before pushing the gates open.

"Budi, flash the torch twice at the car. Then turn it off."

I follow Uncle's instructions, and through the noise

of the rain I hear two car doors slam shut.

"Come on," Uncle says, passing the rucksack to me and hurrying through the gates. I swing the rucksack over my shoulder and follow him towards the container truck. In the darkness it looks like a living thing, long and dark like a huge whale. The factory looms up out of the gloom beyond it, and along one wall, on the other side of the chain-link fence, I see the rows of bins where I found Uncle. Despite everything, I can't help wondering if my poster of Kieran Wakefield is still in one of them.

When we reach the back of the truck, Uncle asks me to shine the torch again, and he starts picking the two padlocks that fasten the back doors. As he works the pins in the first lock I notice a van pulling in through the gates. Its headlights are off, and it rolls into the fenced enclosure without making a sound. It turns and reverses alongside the container truck, parking as close as possible. I recognize the two men who jump out of the driver's cab from the Dragon's house: Bayu and Boaz. They hunch against the rain and lift the shutter on the back of their van. They are wearing the same gloves as me. To start with they haul out a couple of barrels and a few crates, but then people start climbing out of the back. Most of them are men, but every so often a child is lowered into the rain.

The second padlock pops open, and Uncle lifts them both out of their holdings.

"Give me a hand," he says, grasping one of the levers and pulling it to the side.

I unhook the other lever and push with all my strength to prise the doors open.

And then we step back and stare into the truck. I shine the torch on stacks and stacks of shoeboxes, hundreds and hundreds of them piled up on wooden pallets and wrapped in plastic.

The Dragon strides across and smirks at the sight.

"Let's make it quick," he says.

Then his brothers start shouting orders, and the strongest men climb into the container truck and push a pallet to the edge. One time I watched a group of ants carry a huge cockroach back to their nest. It looked a lot like this. As each pallet of shoeboxes is transferred across to the van, another person climbs into the container truck. The barrels and crates are lifted in, and Uncle turns to the Dragon beside him.

"Are those all the provisions they have?"

The Dragon shrugs. "Some of them won't make it. I never guaranteed anything."

The men keep working. A little girl stands to the side,

her black hair hanging in strands, a sodden blanket clutched in her hand. She stares at the Dragon and his brothers without any fear, and when she looks at me I have to turn away. One of the men helps her into the back of the container. She argues that she doesn't want to go, and I'm glad when her brother or cousin or whoever he is clamps a hand over her mouth and drags her backwards, deeper into the container. I turn the torch off and drop it into my pocket.

It takes about an hour to fill the Dragon's van with pallets. Then Bayu and Boaz close the shutter, climb into the cab and drive away. The men from the van look exhausted, but they clamber into the back of the container and huddle near the remaining pallets at the far end. As the doors close they look out, a dark shape with many glistening eyes.

And then the doors clang shut, and the Dragon swings the levers across and fastens the padlocks through the loops.

I wonder where the container is going, and how long it will take to get there, and who will open it on the other side.

I wonder what they'll find.

But I think I already know.

"Now you can release Elvis," Uncle says. "I want to see him before your crooked brother comes to arrest me. After what I've done for you it's only the right thing to do."

The Dragon stands with his back to us, his gloved hands resting on the container doors. He shakes his head, tutting.

"Aaron," he says, turning round slowly. "You should know by now there's no honour among thieves."

In one smooth movement the Dragon pulls something from his belt. But it's not the knife I'm expecting. It's a revolver, just like the ones the police use.

"I think you knew it would come to this, Aaron. There isn't any other way it could end."

I feel as though my legs might give way at any moment, but Uncle doesn't even flinch at the sight of the gun.

"You can shoot me if you want," he says calmly. "But Budi won't be here to see it."

The Dragon raises his eyebrows and rainwater trickles down his face. "So you want me to shoot him first?" He points the gun at me, and my heart thumps in my chest. This is what it must be like to take the deciding penalty in a Cup Final. It feels as though I'm about to vomit my heart into the puddle in front of me.

"No," Uncle says. "I want you to let him go. He shouldn't be here. He's nothing to do with this. With that." He points at the container truck behind the Dragon.

"I can't do that, I'm afraid," the Dragon says. "He knows too much."

He reaches into his pocket and takes out a mobile phone. The little keypad lights up when he presses a button, and it throws a sickly glow across his face as he lifts it to his ear. He holds the revolver at arm's length, aiming at the space between Uncle and me.

"Brother," the Dragon says. "It's done…" He glances at us. "Yes, bring him here. Do you want me to wait and we'll do all three together? Or should I get these two over with…? Yes, I've got your gun. You'll get the credit, don't worry… Yes, I know…in the back while trying to evade capture. You said that already… Okay. Bye."

He puts the phone back in his pocket.

"Turn around, Aaron," he says.

He knows that we've heard him. When Uncle hesitates the Dragon aims at me. Rain drips from the end of the barrel.

"Do you really want to watch your nephew die?"

Uncle sighs and turns around. He closes his eyes. The Dragon raises the revolver and aims at the back of his head. I turn around too. I can't watch. The rain seems to get heavier, and every drop feels like a bullet against my back.

I close my eyes.

I take a deep breath.

"I'm sorry," I say, but I don't know if Uncle can hear me.

Then there is a click.

My eyes open, and Uncle is no longer beside me. I turn just in time to see the Dragon pull the trigger again. But nothing happens. It just clicks. There must be water in the mechanism. And then Uncle tackles him, slamming the Dragon against the doors of the container truck. They land heavily, splashing into a puddle. The revolver falls to the ground. The Dragon is a much bigger man than Uncle, and as they thrash around he manages to pin Uncle down. He pushes his face into the puddle and reaches for something tucked into his belt.

It glints in the darkness.

I rush forward without thinking, shoving the Dragon before he can bring the knife down. Uncle gasps for breath, wiping the muddy water from his face. The Dragon swings an arm back and his bejewelled hand catches me on the side of the head.

For a moment there's nothing. Then all I can see is the rain as it falls towards my face out of the blackness. From somewhere nearby come the sounds of grunting, splashing. Gargling. I try to sit up but my head is heavy, and the ground seems to tilt. I roll onto my side and force myself onto all fours. I retch but nothing comes out. The world stops rocking. My vision settles, but the puddle beneath my face seems to be turning red. I look up.

The Dragon lies on his back. His domed stomach is still. A knife sticks out of his chest. Beside him my uncle struggles to get to his feet. He clutches at his ribs and shuffles around the side of the truck. I manage to stand and stagger over to him, but he falls before I can catch him. He twists around and sits with his back against one of the truck's wheels.

"You've got to get out of here, Budi," he says, wincing against the pain. He peels his hand away from his side and I see the cut across his ribs.

A cut like that won't stop bleeding. Not without a bucket of coconut butter.

"But first you've got to get those people out of the truck. There's a pair of bolt cutters in the rucksack. Use them to cut the padlocks."

I open the rucksack to find the bolt cutters, but all I

can see are multicoloured bundles of paper. In the darkness it's difficult to make out what they are, but when I take one out I realize exactly what it is.

"They're not all for you," Uncle says, trying to smile.

I just stare at him.

"What?" he says. "You didn't think I'd miss an opportunity to rob that pig, did you? Once a thief, always a thief."

He laughs, but doubles over immediately. I look back into the open rucksack.

"But there must be millions in here," I say. "Millions and millions."

"Well, everyone in the truck paid a million, and I think it's only fair they get that back. But the rest is for you, Budi. Do whatever you want with it. I've heard that football academies can be expensive places."

I blink away the tears. I'm holding the bag that could change my life. No more days at the factory. No more blows from the *rotan*. No more fake, leaky boots. Just days of playing football at the academy in new boots. Real boots. The same boots that Kieran Wakefield wears. Playing my way up through the academy and into La Liga.

I realize I've got to tell my uncle something before it's too late.

"Grandma died today," I say. "The only reason I gave you over to the Dragon was so that she wouldn't have to choose between you and Dad. I'm sorry, Uncle. I thought you'd get to see her. I thought we could all be together. I was just trying to do the right thing."

"You did," he says, closing his eyes. "And I did get to see her. I visited her this morning, after the earthquake." He smiles. "I think she thought I was Elvis. She just said, 'My son, my son!' and hugged me. She never could tell us apart as children. I got to hold her hand. I got to say goodbye. I told your mother not to tell you that I'd visited – I didn't want her to know about all this. I just wanted to make things right. I think she understood."

I nod, looking down at the rucksack.

"Thank you," I say.

Uncle doesn't respond. He just sits there smiling. I say it again, louder this time.

"Thank you."

But Uncle doesn't respond.

I sit on the wet ground, cradling the rucksack. I dig down to the bottom of it for the bolt cutters, but before I can bring them out a pair of headlights swings through the gates. I scurry around the back of the container and press myself flat against the doors. The Dragon's body is

270

so close and everything about it – the gold chains on his motionless chest, his slack, bejewelled hands, his still-open eyes – urges me to run. But I don't move. I take a deep breath and push myself closer to the truck as the sound of an engine draws nearer.

Then it cuts out and I hear a door slam.

Someone spits.

"Get out," a voice says, and I know it's the Chief Inspector. Another door slams. "Move it!"

And then I hear something that makes me wish the Dragon had shot me in the back of the head. I hear Dad sobbing, and I know he's just seen his brother for the first time in ten years. And his brother is dead.

"Aaron," he says, as though he's pleading with him to wake up, to change his mind. "Aaron."

"Shut up," the Chief Inspector says. "You haven't seen the worst of it yet."

Dad cries out as though someone is torturing him.

"Oh, no!" he sobs. "Not my boy. Please, no." And I am filled with a rage like I have never felt before. I always thought I hated Uston and Barcelona and Lazaro Celestino, but now I know what hatred really is. It's a burning, seething venom that poisons your blood and makes you fearless.

I spot the Dragon's revolver on the floor and swoop down to pick it up. It feels cold and heavy in my hand. The Chief Inspector's footsteps come closer. It sounds as though Dad is being dragged forward. I wait until they must only be a couple of steps away before spinning round the side of the container and pointing the gun in the Chief Inspector's face.

He almost slips over as he tries to back away. He lets go of Dad's arm and raises his hands in front of his face.

"Don't shoot!" he says. "You don't know what you're doing. You can't shoot a police officer!"

"No," I say, shaking my head. "But I can shoot you."

He smirks as though he is about to dare me, but then he glances over my shoulder and his eyes widen. He must have seen the Dragon's body. He takes another step backwards.

"What have you done?" he asks.

I take a step forward, hoping he won't call my bluff.

"By tomorrow everyone will know how corrupt you are, and the Dragon won't be around to protect you. They'll hunt you down and send you to Nusa Kambangan. I'm giving you a chance to run. Go and tell your brothers that the Dragon is dead, and don't ever come back here again."

I cock the revolver and aim it straight at the Chief Inspector's heart.

This time he doesn't smirk. He just turns and runs, slipping in the mud as he fumbles with the car door. I keep the revolver aimed at him until the car swerves through the gates and races out of sight.

I drop the gun. Dad rushes over and hugs me. I look at him properly for the first time. He looks awful. He mustn't have slept since he was taken. He hugs me again and holds me for a long time. The rain starts to ease.

Eventually Dad goes over to Uncle and crouches by his side.

"He just wanted to make things right," I say.

Dad nods. "I know." He bows his head, resting a hand on Uncle's shoulder. "A mother and a brother in one day."

Then he looks up at the sky, as though asking Allah for an explanation.

But the sky just spits.

I take the bolt cutters from the rucksack and break both padlocks on the container. The people inside are surprised to see me, and when they see the Dragon lying in a pool of blood, a knife sticking out of his chest, they look horrified. But I don't think any of them can look at the Dragon for long without realizing they have one less thing to worry about in Jakarta.

They shuffle out one by one, and as they pass I give them a roll of cash each. I help the little girl with the blanket down and she gives me a hug.

"Thank you," she says. And the last of the rage seeps out of my veins.

Some of the men look down at the body and pat me on the shoulder, like I'm the hero. Like I stepped up and scored the final penalty. But it wasn't me.

When they pass my uncle they bow their heads and leave in silence.

In the end it's just me and Dad and the rucksack, still heavy with bundles of cash. Dad stands up and puts his arm across my shoulders. The rain finally stops.

"We've got to leave him here, haven't we?" I ask. "They'll never stop looking for him."

"Yes, son." Dad sighs. "There's nothing else we can do."

We stand side by side in silence. Then, without saying a word, we turn and make our way home.

Someone is waiting at the end of the street. The name on the back of his shirt reads: *B LM NTE*. He sits on a chunk of concrete, knocking a stone from one foot to the other. As we get nearer he glances over his shoulder and stands up.

I nod at Rochy. He nods back.

Dad reaches out and puts a hand on Rochy's shoulder, squeezing it slightly.

Rochy lowers his head.

"I'll leave you two to talk," Dad says. "I need to see my wife."

We don't say anything until Dad is almost home. He shuffles like a much older man, gazing at the destruction all around him. Then Rochy looks at me and frowns.

"What have you been doing?"

I look down at my soaked, dirty, bloody clothes.

"Slaying a dragon. It's a long story."

He nods and we fall silent.

"I just came to say goodbye," Rochy says, looking at his shoes. "I think I've got some relatives near Surabaya so I'm going to head that way. They've got a farm, I think. There's nothing left for me here."

My heart falls into my stomach. Just when I thought the wound was finally closing, Rochy tears it open again.

"You can't leave, Rochy, and you can't work on a farm. You're a genius."

He smiles. "I don't really have a choice."

For a moment I think he's right. What choice does he have? Then I realize that for once *I* have a choice. And I could choose to give Rochy a choice.

My fingers tighten around the strap on the rucksack. It seems to get heavier as I stand here, as if it's filling with all the things I want, all the things it could give me. I look around at the broken buildings, the empty lives – the ruins of everything. I watch my dad, only just reaching the apartment now, looking broken, looking beaten. The rucksack gets heavier and heavier until I'm sure the Bernabéu – the world – must be inside it.

Then I look at Rochy – jobless, homeless, alone – and I let out a long, slow breath.

"Here," I say, offering him the rucksack.

"What's in it?" he asks.

"Just take it. It's for you."

He takes the rucksack and opens it.

"Where did you get this?" he asks, taking out a roll of notes.

"My uncle stole it from the Dragon. He told me to do whatever I want with it. And I want to give it to you."

Rochy starts to shake his head. "I can't take this," he says. "You could do so much with it. You could afford to train at the academy. It could be the first step to Madrid. I can't take it."

He holds the bag out to me but I don't reach for it. I put my hands in my pockets.

"Go back to school, Rochy. Start again."

I walk away before he has time to argue, before he has time to notice me crying. I just leave him standing among the rubble, clutching a bag full of money.

When I reach my apartment I look back. Rochy stands at the end of the road, the rucksack hanging by his side.

I pat my chest where the Real Madrid badge should be and make my hands into the shape of a heart.

I hold the heart above my head.

Then I step through the door.

# TODAY, TOMORROW AND FOREVER

The next day I go to the factory.

There are quite a few empty seats, and I can tell the foreman is really angry about the earthquake. He paces along each row with his *rotan*, making sure we don't talk, don't fall asleep, don't fall behind. But he leaves me alone. He stares at me a lot, just like everyone else, but he doesn't shout at me once. I think maybe he read the newspaper this morning.

All the papers are full of stories about how one of Indonesia's most wanted criminals was found dead with one of Jakarta's most notorious landlords next to a half-empty container truck.

This is the other thing the foreman is angry about. A group of white men showed up this morning and spent a long time going round the factory with the foreman. I've never seen so many white people outside of a television before. There were almost enough to make a football team. The foreman was sweating like Elvis and kept mopping his forehead with his handkerchief. He looked glad to see them leave.

Annisa, the same girl as before, sits in Rochy's place. I ask her whether she knows the El Clásico result. But she doesn't. She just shrugs and refuses to make eye contact. I think she might be a hopeless case.

During my break I sit in the canteen, staring into my tray of rice and "Sauce of the Day". It's the same sauce every day – it never changes. I scrape the grey rice into little piles and move them around the tray. No one sits at my table, they just glance over and whisper to each other. When the buzzer goes, I head back to my station with an empty stomach and make some more football boots.

The next day there is another story in the newspaper about a senior police officer who is now a missing person.

The next day there is another story in the newspaper about a senior police officer who is now a wanted person.

The day after that two men are arrested with a van full of stolen football boots. The white men make sure they end up on a boat to Nusa Kambangan. When they eventually find the Chief Inspector, hiding in a shack in the slums, they put him on the boat as well.

There are no stories about a teenage boy being found with a rucksack full of money. I make Dad read the entire newspaper out loud every evening, week after week, to make sure.

Uston is really annoyed at Rochy for disappearing. He still hasn't forgiven him for punching him in the face.

"If he ever shows his face in this square again I'll knock him out," he says.

"It's not technically a square," I say. "It's a quadrilateral quadrangle."

"Do you want a punch as well?"

He curls his right hand into a fist and waves it in my face.

"Come on," I say. "Let's play."

Now that Rochy is gone I have to play two-on-one against Uston and Widodo. We pretend I've had a player sent off. I don't mind. It means I have to work harder. It's what all the professional players do. If you can win when you're outnumbered, then one day you'll be a champion. That's a fact.

So long as you don't forget how to pass the ball.

When Fachry, Uston and Widodo aren't around, I

practise kick-ups. Sometimes when I'm tired and bored and my legs ache, and it feels as though the Bernabéu is a million miles away (instead of just 7,500), I go to the academy and watch them play through the fence. Sometimes the groundskeeper is there, and we watch together. Sometimes there's no one at all, so I just close my eyes and breathe the smell of grass and feel the glare of floodlights on my face. Then I go home and practise some more.

Without Rochy's television I lose track of Real Madrid's season. Uston tries to convince me that Real Madrid are in the relegation zone and Kieran Wakefield has been sold to a team I've never even heard of for 100,000 rupiah. But I know he's lying. And it just makes me want to beat him even more.

After a few months it stops raining, and the factory goes from being really, really loud and really hot to really loud and really, really hot. Annisa still doesn't like football, but sometimes we talk about other things. I suppose she's not all bad.

Since Rochy left I have to walk home by myself. I usually practise my skills by dribbling a stone back to my apartment. With stones you have to concentrate extra hard because otherwise you can lose them down a drain.

It helps if you commentate as well.

"Wakefield goes past one…and another…he's unstoppable! Just the keeper to beat—"

Suddenly a leg flicks out and drags the stone away from me.

"But Belmonte takes it off him and slams it into the net! *Goooooooal!*"

The stone pings off a metal shutter and the person who kicked it pulls his shirt over his head. It isn't until he uncovers his face that I realize who it is.

"Rochy!" I shout. I hug him and don't even feel embarrassed. Footballers do it all the time, so you know it's okay. "What are you doing here? Where's your Manchester United shirt?"

He looks down at the T-shirt he's wearing – it's grey with a planet printed on the front. For some reason he doesn't seem as tall any more.

"Well, it was getting a bit small for me, and all the letters were peeling off. Besides, I'm not a Manchester United fan."

"I like this T-shirt better," I say, smiling. "You're fired, by the way. I forgot to tell you."

Rochy laughs. "Well, you can tell the foreman that I quit."

"What are you doing instead?"

"I'm back at school," he says, and he can't keep the smile from his face. But then it falls.

"Did you hear that Atlético won the league?"

My mouth drops open. "What? At least it wasn't Barca, I suppose."

Rochy nods and squints into the setting sun.

"Do you want to come to mine for dinner?" I ask. "Dad's got a new job so there should be enough to go around."

"It's okay, I've already eaten. I'm working as a waiter and they give me my meals. It's a pretty good deal. Sometimes, white people eat at the restaurant and just give me money for nothing when they leave. Especially when I speak English."

"Cool." It sounds like one of Rochy's dubious facts to me. "Do you want to play football instead?"

"No, I'm going home. I want to see if anything's changed. I haven't been back since...well, since then."

I nod. I understand. But it hurts.

"I've got a surprise for you though," Rochy says.

"Really? What is it?"

"If I told you it wouldn't be much of a surprise, would it? Just meet me at the factory in a couple of hours and I'll show you."

"Okay, I'll be there." I give Rochy another hug. He doesn't mind. Like I said, it's good practice for goal celebrating.

I rush home to tell my parents that Rochy is back, and they're both glad to hear he's at school. Mum makes a delicious curry with garlic rice for dinner, and as soon as I've finished the last mouthful I jump up and run to the door.

"Where are you going?" Dad asks.

"Rochy's planned a surprise. I don't want to be late."

"You'll get indigestion if you don't slow down," Mum says. "What time are you coming back?"

"I don't know, but I'll be careful!"

I'm already out the door and running down the street by the time my parents say goodbye. Within thirty seconds I have indigestion and have to slow down to a walk. The air is warm and still, and everything about the city seems lazy. The people who are in the street look like they've got nowhere to go; a lot of buildings are still just piles of rubble. When I finally arrive at the factory my stomach cramps have gone, and Rochy is waiting for me on the kerb.

"Okay," he says. "Are you ready?"

I nod.

"Let's go."

I ask him where we're going but he won't tell me anything. We walk for a long time – mile after mile – and even though my shoes split weeks ago they still get tighter and tighter the further we walk. Eventually, we reach roads that are clean and well marked, and Rochy asks someone for directions to a place I've never heard of.

"When are you going to tell me what we're doing?" I ask. "My feet hurt."

"I'm not. We're just going to get there and then you'll see what it is."

We pass big houses that are set back from the road and surrounded by smooth concrete walls. It's like the earthquake never happened. I stop at the tall iron gates of one house but Rochy tells me that we need to keep moving. There is a shiny car in the driveway, and flowers planted in tubs by the front door.

"So what are you doing at school?" I ask. "Are you on the space programme yet?"

Rochy laughs. "Not exactly, but I'm learning some pretty interesting stuff. Did you know that there might be an infinite number of parallel universes?"

I don't even know where to start with that question.

"What?"

"Some people think our universe might be just one of countless variations. There could be millions and millions of parallel universes, each one with its own reality. Why have you stopped? We need to keep moving."

I stop rubbing my head and start walking again. "What?"

"Each universe is just a replica of this one, except little things are different."

"Different how?"

"Well, in one variant, Indonesia might have won every World Cup there's ever been. In another, you might live in one of these big houses. In another, Kieran Wakefield might play for Barcelona."

I shake my head. He's taken it too far.

"I don't think your teacher knows what he's talking about."

Rochy laughs again. "But the exciting thing is that if there are an infinite number of universes, that means there are an infinite number of possibilities. Nothing is impossible."

"But how do you know which universe you're in? How do you know what's possible?"

We both stop and Rochy holds out his arms.

"You don't – you just have to work it out for yourself. Come on, it's not much further."

We set off again. My feet are really starting to get sore. I'm just about to give up hope of ever finding out what the surprise is when Rochy cuts down a pathway between two walls. He lifts a finger to his lips and I follow him in silence. We stop at a wooden side gate and Rochy looks along the alley in both directions. Then he interlocks his fingers and crouches down beside the gate.

"What are you doing?" I ask.

"Shhh!" he says. "Keep your voice down. What does it look like I'm doing? I'm helping you over."

"But why?"

"You'll see. Now, come on."

"But what if I get caught?"

"No one will see you if you keep quiet and stick to the shadows. Hurry up!"

I place one foot on Rochy's hands and grip the top of the gate. As Rochy stands up I swing my leg over the top and drop down on the other side. I land in a crouching position on a lawn of thick, cool grass. There is a tree in the middle of what I soon realize is not a park but someone's garden. I hear Rochy scramble over the gate and land beside me.

"What are we doing here?" I ask. "You're going to get us in trouble."

"Calm down. Just stick with me and you'll be fine. Come on, we're not finished yet."

Rochy scurries across the lawn towards the house. I have never seen a house as big as this one, except for in the movies. I run after Rochy, who kneels behind a low wall that separates the lawn from a path that runs around the house.

"Get down," he says.

I dive onto my stomach and wriggle the rest of the way like some kind of commando.

"Who lives here?" I whisper.

"A businessman who eats at the restaurant sometimes," he says, grinning. "From Spain."

"So what are we doing here?"

I can hear my heart pounding in my ears, and I worry that it might be loud enough for someone else to hear. Rochy peers over the wall and smiles.

"Have a look through the window," he says.

Slowly, I raise my head above the wall. The room beyond the window is bathed in green light, and it takes me a moment to understand what I'm looking at.

"That's got to be the biggest television in the world," I whisper. "No wonder the house is so big – it has to be, otherwise nothing would fit."

Then there is a close-up on the screen. Hair swept back. Brilliant white shirt. Yellow and orange boots.

I suddenly realize what we're doing in someone's garden.

"Real Madrid made it to the Champions League final!" I blurt out.

Rochy's hand clamps over my mouth, but when I look at him he's smiling.

"And you'll never guess who they're playing," he says.

I look back at the screen. There is another close-up.

Lazaro Celestino – the most overrated player in the world – darts between a triangle of cones in the dreaded red and blue shirt of the enemy: *Barcelona*.

"Come on," Rochy says, "let's sit on the wall."

On a long sofa in front of the television, a man sits with his back to us. When the adverts come on he scratches his head and drinks something out of a green bottle. Even though I can only see the back of his head, he somehow looks lonely.

We're just in time, because when the adverts end the players walk out onto the pitch and the game begins. The screen is so big that everything is really clear, and it doesn't matter that we're watching from the garden. When I look across at Rochy he is so transfixed by the game that he doesn't notice me, and I watch the little green rectangles dancing in his eyes.

Barcelona score in the first half even though Real Madrid are the much better team. The businessman must be a Barcelona fan because he jumps up and spills his drink everywhere when the ball hits the back of the net. They do so many action replays I start to feel sick. It gets worse every time. Slow-motion Lazaro Celestino should be banned.

At half-time we are one–nil down. The man on the sofa gets up and leaves the room but comes back a few minutes later with another green bottle. I imagine what's going on in the changing room.

*The players sit around the edge of the room on benches. They sip water from sports bottles and pull their socks up. One of them is receiving treatment from the team doctor.*

*The manager stands in the middle of the room in a suit, pointing to a board covered with arrows and crosses.*

*"Belmonte, you need to run at their defenders. Draw out players to create a space behind for Bello and Tapia on the overlap. Noguerra, Ochoa – you need to move the ball faster. You should be looking to release Wakefield as soon as you get the ball. He's too quick for their back line and he'll cause them lots of problems.*

"I'm also making a change. Rubio, you're coming off."

The manager looks around the dressing room.

"Budi, get your boots on. I want you to play in the centre – stop Barca from getting at our defence, and support Wakefield when we're on the attack."

I look across at Kieran Wakefield. He winks at me.

"We can still turn this around!' the manager says, clapping his hands. "This is your moment! And that trophy is yours for the taking! Hala Madrid!"

Every player gets to his feet. The dressing room echoes with the clapping of hands and the clacking of studs on the floor. We jog along the tunnel and out onto the pitch. The crowd chant and cheer, and thousands of camera flashes make the stadium sparkle like a jewel.

Rochy nudges me in the ribs.

"Here we go."

The second half kicks off and Real Madrid are constantly on the attack. We have shot after shot, but somehow the ball stays out of the net. When it gets to seventy minutes gone and we still haven't scored I start biting my fingernails. When it gets to eighty minutes gone I have to watch through my fingers.

The clock reaches ninety minutes and we move into injury time.

And then it happens.

One second there's nothing.

No hope.

And then a brilliant flash of white, like light across a needle, as Kieran Wakefield slips between two defenders and Belmonte flicks the ball into the gap behind them.

I jump to my feet as every player charges towards the Barcelona goal.

But ahead of them all is Kieran Wakefield.

And no one is fast enough to catch him.

He reaches the ball just inside the penalty area and pulls back his left foot. The goalkeeper steps forward, arms stretched wide, eyes fixed on the ball, and I swear my heart stops beating in that moment. My breath catches in my chest. I can't take my eyes off his left boot as it swings towards the ball.

I don't see the defender, lunging in from behind. Not until he's crashed through Wakefield's standing leg and sent him tumbling to the ground. But Rochy must see him, because his hand slaps over my mouth before the scream even reaches my throat, before Wakefield even hits the grass. I wriggle and try to get away from him, but he won't let go.

"Budi!" he hisses in my ear. "Shut up or we'll miss

what happens next. He's pointing to the spot – look."

Rochy is right. The referee already has the red card in his hand as he reaches the box. And he's pointing to the penalty spot. Players from both teams surround the defender and shout and shove at each other. Kieran Wakefield gets to his feet, wincing as he bends his knee and a trickle of blood seeps into his white sock.

But he's reaching for the ball in the goalkeeper's hand.

And the goalkeeper gives it to him like he's handing over the Champions League trophy.

It takes a long time for the rest of the players to leave the penalty area – and even longer for the sent-off defender to leave the pitch – but eventually it's just Kieran Wakefield and the goalkeeper. With everyone gone, there is a close-up of Wakefield holding the football. He looks tired. Exhausted. Like he might only have one kick left in him. I reach out and put my hand against the window. But there's no tingle, no shock. It's just cold glass. Kieran Wakefield starts to blur, but I blink it away. Not in front of Rochy. I know there is a universe where he equalizes, where we go on to win. But how do you know which one? And what if this isn't it? I blink it away again. But what if this isn't it?

I lower myself onto the wall. My fingers leave a smudge on the glass.

Kieran Wakefield steps forward and bends over the penalty spot. The camera follows the ball as he places it on the white circle of grass between his feet. Sweat drips from his fringe, and a drop of blood falls from his knee and splashes onto the toe of his left boot.

But he doesn't notice.

He just turns and walks to the edge of the box.

Even when he stoops to pull his socks up he still doesn't notice. But the splash of red is all I can see. I look at Rochy and I know he's seen it too, because how could anyone *not* see it? How could anyone ignore it?

"He's got blood on his boots," I whisper. "He's got blood on his boots."

And I look at the three little scars across my fingertip, and I can taste the blood at the back of my throat.

But Kieran Wakefield just puts his hands on his hips.

Puffs his cheeks out.

And waits for the whistle.

The keeper stands on his line, waving his arms like he's about to fly. With every sweep he seems to get bigger, until his fingertips brush the posts and his head scrapes the underside of the bar.

And Kieran Wakefield suddenly seems a long way out.

The space between the penalty spot and the goal

stretches and stretches until the goal is nothing more than a speck on the far side of a vast ocean. Wakefield looks small and lonely – marooned – like a little boy who can't possibly make it; the keeper is too big, the goal is too small, and the whole crowd – the whole *world* – is against him.

It's impossible.

But then the camera flicks to a close-up of his face, and he's staring so hard at the ball I realize he can't see the keeper towering up like an impossibly tall palm tree. He can't see the impassable ocean that's opened up between them.

He can't see the impossible, because impossible is nothing.

All he can see is the football, waiting for one final kick.

And then the referee blows his whistle.

And Wakefield starts his run-up.

And Rochy holds my hand.

It's now or never.

And I know, I just *know*, it's now.

# Introducing MITCH JOHNSON

**MITCH JOHNSON** studied English Literature with Creative Writing at the University of East Anglia. Mitch now works as a bookseller at Waterstones, Norwich, and writes in his spare time. Mitch loves reading and, like Budi, is a big football fan (although his chances of turning professional are considerably slimmer).

"A must-read for fans of Mal Peet."
**Tom Palmer, author of FOOTBALL ACADEMY**

"To grow up with stories like these is the beginning of finding another world, lying at our feet."
**Khalid Abdalla, star of THE KITE RUNNER**

"Fast-paced, funny and involving. Mitch Johnson is a brilliant writer." **Anjali Joseph, author of SARASWATI PARK**

# Q&A with MITCH

### Mitch, we'd love to hear a little more about what inspired you to write this story?

The spark for *Kick* came when I was working in a sports shop and found a crumpled energy gel sachet in a shoebox between a brand new pair of football boots. I couldn't help but imagine who had left it there, and what kind of working environment would force someone to consume a product normally used by endurance athletes. The idea crystallized a few weeks later as I channel-hopped between "Match of the Day" and a programme protesting against the use of sweatshops. The outrageous disparity between top-flight footballers and garment workers compelled me to do something about it, and I began work on *Kick* the same evening.

### What research did you do while you were writing *Kick*?

Researching sweatshops is a difficult business. Companies spend huge sums of money to ensure we only see what they want us to see: their immaculate, branded products. However, there are lots of authors, charities, investigative journalists and documentary makers reporting on working and living conditions in the garment industry, and these offer invaluable insights into the lives behind the logos. Having never been to Jakarta, I made Indonesia and its capital a focus of my reading, and drew on an earlier visit to Mumbai for a sense of the chaos of an Asian metropolis. While Jakarta and Mumbai are vastly different places, the trip allowed me to experience many things – the oppressive heat, the endless traffic jams, the stifling pollution, the round-the-clock cacophony, the masses of people, the explosion of cultures, the wealthy living alongside the destitute – that are characteristic of both cities, and would later help me to visualize Budi's world.

## Did you ever find it hard putting yourself in Budi's shoes?

My life is not like Budi's. I do not know what it is like to go hungry, or to work in fear of violence, or to live next door to destitution. I have never set foot inside a sweatshop. And yet, we also have everything in common. To have dreams, to search for happiness, to want a better life for your family – these are fundamental human traits that we all share. And when you focus on our inherent similarities – rather than the circumstantial differences that separate us – it becomes so much easier to see things through the eyes of others. Budi's life is tough, and there were many occasions when I did not want to confront it any longer. But problems rarely get better by pretending they don't exist, and I took heart from the people for whom sweatshops are an everyday reality. My hope is that this book will make these people more visible and kickstart an important conversation. Exploitative labour practices are a global problem, but empathizing with its victims is a crucial step towards change; if you felt the heat of the factory, flinched at the swish of the *rotan*, or bled a little bit on the inside while reading *Kick*, you are already part of the solution.

## Which football team do you support?

Growing up, I was a huge Newcastle United fan. Supporting Newcastle United is the polar opposite of being a glory supporter; there is nothing but heartbreak and despair. Nowadays I am a lot kinder to myself and enjoy being a neutral, although I followed Real Madrid closely while working on *Kick*. Cheering them on to two Champions League titles was a fantastic experience – especially as both finals were won against Atlético Madrid.

## What's the best goal you've ever scored?

That's easy! I only ever scored once for my childhood team, Billing United, and it was an absolute worldie! The ball came out to me on the edge of the box after a corner and I hit it first time, lobbing the keeper. The crowd (about a dozen parents) went wild (clapped politely). As a defender who never, ever scored, I didn't have a celebration so I think I just ran around a bit. It obviously affected my defensive duties because we went on to lose 4-2.

## Budi's grandma tells him amazing stories; were there any stories that inspired you growing up?

My favourite book as a child was *The Phantom Tollbooth* by Norton Juster – I love the way Juster plays with logic and language, twisting the everyday into the magical and making the rational seem nonsensical. I loved it so much that the school librarian let me keep the copy I'd borrowed! My grandparents also inspired me; aspects of Grandma's character were drawn from my own doting grandmother, and my grandfather always had lots of stories from his time at sea. I always loved to hear their stories – grandparents are real-life time-travellers!

## What can we expect from you next, Mitch?

My next book will be about a boy called Oscar and how his family is pushed to breaking point by the after-effects of war. It will be similar to *Kick* in the sense that I'm tackling a serious issue with warmth and humour, so you can expect video games and a militarized pug, as well as tough decisions and lots of bravery.

Amnesty International UK endorses *Kick* because it upholds and illuminates many children's rights. Children have the right to be protected from work that harms you and is bad for your health and education. If you work, you have the right to be safe and to be paid fairly.

Amnesty International is a movement of millions of ordinary people around the world standing up for humanity and human rights. We try to protect people wherever justice, fairness, freedom and truth are denied.

Human rights are universal and all children and adults have them, no matter who we are or where we live. Human rights are rooted in values that include truth, justice, freedom, safety and equality. They help us to live lives that are fair and truthful, free from abuse, fear and hardship. But they are often abused and we need to be alert and to stand up for ourselves and for other people. We can all help to make the world a better place.

You can stand up for human rights too:

• Take action for individuals at risk around the world at www.amnesty.org.uk/actions

• Find out how to start a Youth Group in your school or community at www.amnesty.org.uk/groups/youth

• Join the Junior Urgent Action network at www.amnesty.org.uk/jua

If you are a teacher or librarian, please use our many free educational resources at www.amnesty.org.uk/education

Amnesty International UK,
The Human Rights Action Centre, 17-25 New Inn Yard, London EC2A 3EA
Tel: 020 7033 1500
Email: sct@amnesty.org.uk
www.amnesty.org.uk

# Acknowledgements

Writing is a team sport, and there are so many people in need of thanks for getting *Kick* to where it is today.

To my parents, David and Christine, for your encouragement, support and love. To my brothers, Vince and Howard, for the countless hours of street football and FIFA/ Pro Evo/International Superstar Soccer 64 – those were the days! (Mum and Dad, sorry for turning the garden into a dust bowl during our attempts to recreate World Cup glory.)

I have been lucky enough to have many brilliant teachers over the years, but special thanks must go to Karen Ellis for pushing me to follow a creative path, and making me feel like a writer when I was not.

To Claire Griffiths, for being so receptive when I first mentioned the idea behind *Kick* during one of our supervision sessions. To Jay Willis, B.J. Epstein and Jacob Huntley for reading *Kick* when it really wasn't ready to be seen – your feedback improved the novel immensely. Thanks also to Josh Judd, who has always taken an inexplicable – some would say unnatural – interest in my creative endeavours.

Many thanks to my fantastic agent, Felicity Trew, for being Budi's biggest fan from the first whistle; because of your passion, I know *Kick* will always have the home advantage, wherever it goes.

I cannot imagine a more energetic, enthusiastic team than the one I became a part of at Usborne. Thanks to Rebecca Hill and Becky Walker for your editorial guidance and for understanding what I was trying to achieve. Above all, thank you for believing in Budi and me – we will never stop kicking. To Sarah Stewart and Anne Finnis for being the eagle-eyed coaches who picked up on my mistakes along the way. To Amy Dobson, Stevie Hopwood, Alesha Bonser, Sarah Connell and Liz Scott for all the marketing and PR goodness. To Katharine Millichope for designing a beautiful cover, and Sarah Cronin for threading this beauty throughout the novel. Thank you to everyone at Usborne; you have made my dream come true.

Finally, my eternal gratitude goes to Harriet, who is definitely not a glory supporter. Thank you for remaining undeterred by the defeats, for always having a team talk ready, and for helping me to celebrate the victories. I hope this book is some consolation for all those evenings and weekends it forced us to spend apart. You were always on my mind.

# An Indonesian glossary

Budi and his friends are Indonesian, and live in one of the poorer areas of Jakarta, the capital city of Indonesia. They speak Indonesian (known as Bahasa Indonesia). There are several words in the novel which are in Indonesian, and whose English translation can be found here.

**Anjing** – dog

**Bapak** – father (or respectful term for an older man)

**Berak** – to poo

**Ibu** – mother (or respectful term for an older woman)

**kain** – stiff cloth wrapped around the waist, usually worn by women in Indonesian villages, or by the very traditional

**Kurang ajar** – literally "less educated", but used to mean "idiot"

**Martabak** – sweet or savoury stuffed pancakes

**Nenek** – grandmother

**Nusa Kambangan** – an Indonesian island, which houses several maximum security prisons

**Pemulung** – scavenger / rubbish picker

**Rendang** – spicy beef curry

**Rotan** – cane

**Sirih** – betel; a plant which is chewed for pleasure

**Tiga, dua, satu** – three, two, one

**Tikus** – rat

**Wajan** – wok